A lonely bear shifter meets his mate. She's running for her life and doesn't have time for romance.

Pregnant Jackie Breton just escaped from a corrupt feline pack intent on selling her half-shifter baby to the highest bidder. She's smart, independent, and has a desperate plan to keep her baby safe: Get away from the pride as fast and far as possible.

Trevor Hammond, prehistoric bear shifter, has been rejected by everyone in his life for... being born, basically. Well, except for the beloved aunt who raised him. He's built a career as an independent trucker, but life would be much better with someone he can hold in his arms and claim as his own.

When Jackie meets Trevor at a truck stop, his bear demands he help her. His aunt even calls with a dire warning: Get Jackie to the magical sanctuary town in Wyoming before she's killed.

Jackie thinks he's sexy as hell, but too good to be true. She doesn't trust shifters. With the feline pride hot on her trail, however, Trevor and the quirky town of Kotoyeesinay might be her only chance for survival. Even Trevor's indomitable bear may be no match for the dangerous enemy seeking retribution.

Discover the secret world of magic and true mates in **Shifter Mate Magic**, the first book in USA TODAY bestselling author Carol Van Natta's fun, action-filled, steamy-hot Ice Age Shifters™ series.

ALSO BY CAROL VAN NATTA

Paranormal Romance

- Shifter Mate Magic (Ice Age Shifters #1)
- Shift of Destiny (Ice Age Shifters #2)

- In Graves Below (Magic, NM)

Space Opera Romance - Central Galactic Concordance Series

- Last Ship Off Polaris-G (Novella)
- Overload Flux (Book 1)
- Minder Rising (Book 2)
- Zero Flux (Novella)
- Pico's Crush (Book 3)
- Pet Trade (Novella)
- Jumper's Hope (Book 4)
- Spark Transform (Book 5)
- Central Galactic Concordance Set (Books 1-3)

Retro Science Fiction Comedy

- Hooray for Holopticon

SHIFTER MATE MAGIC

ICE AGE SHIFTERS BOOK 1

CAROL VAN NATTA

Shifter Mate Magic
(Ice Age Shifters Book 1)

Ice Age Shifters™ is a trademark of Carol Van Natta

Cover and logo design by Amanda Kelsey of Razzle Dazzle Design

Arctotherium illustration by Sam Salas

Published by Chavanch Press

Copyright © 2018 by Carol Van Natta

All rights reserved.

1

J ackie Breton needed to pee in the worst way.

Being five months pregnant meant stopping at every back-road truck stop and gas station, and sometimes behind bushes because her bladder was now the size of a damn walnut. Constant vibration from the motorcycle didn't help.

The faded billboard for Otto's Truck Stop, Take Next Right, enticed her, even though she really wanted to get through Cheyenne before it got too dark to find the highway that would take her east. Rural roads didn't have streetlights. She'd had her fill of dusty back roads and oblivious drivers in smelly diesel pickup trucks. A sharp kick from the baby inside her belly confirmed her decision. She slowed the bike and turned and was gratified to see her destination right away.

Otto's was bigger than she'd imagined, with dozens of long-haul semis, recreational vehicles, and pickup trucks in the sprawling parking lot. The crowd gave her pause, but not enough to turn away. She found a place to park near the front of the main building. The window decorations carried the western wildlife theme into the realm of kitschy, but she liked it.

As she deployed the kickstand and turned off the engine, her bladder spasmed, meaning she had to wait agonizing seconds for the urge to subside, or she'd leak, which would be too utterly embarrassing. She tightened her gloved fists on her thighs and willed the spasm to go away.

When she was sure she had control again, she took off her gloves and shoved them into her jacket pocket, then pulled the key and pocketed it, too. She stomped to get the circulation going in her unexpectedly rubbery legs as she took her backpack off the rail and shouldered it.

After a moment's hesitation, she slid her homemade weapon from the closest saddlebag into the pocket of her loose cargo jeans. Just because the brightly lit convenience store section seemed inviting and friendly didn't make it safe. She'd learned that lesson and so many others the hard way.

She pulled off the helmet, then slipped the re-snapped strap over her arm like a purse, albeit one with a hand-painted flaming skull. She'd been lucky to find a helmet close to her size in the thrift store. Its dusty face shield sported tiny scars from pebbles and splats from insects that would have been in her face if she hadn't been wearing it. The motorcycle's front fairing and windshield didn't block everything.

The ill-fitting leather jacket and heavy denim felt like a furnace now that she was standing in the dry summer heat of twilight, but she wouldn't be there long enough to make it worth her time to do more than unzip the jacket. She guessed she had forty-five minutes until sunset.

Outdoor speakers blared the upbeat country song about an achy-breaky heart. An errant breeze felt good on her sweat plastered short hair, but the mixed smells of oil and gas threatened a return of the awful morning sickness she'd endured for the first sixteen weeks of her pregnancy. She hurried inside.

At the counter, she caught the attention of the clerk. "Restrooms?"

The bony blonde woman with too much makeup over her acne pointed toward the back. "Look for the orange signs. You gotta buy something if you use 'em."

Jackie nodded and walked quickly, following the arrows. Luckily, she didn't have to wait in line or share the facilities. After the blessed relief of peeing, she used soap and water from the sink to make herself look as presentable as possible under the circumstances. Her light brown skin already made her stand out, because the farther north she'd traveled, the fewer people she'd seen who looked like her. She threw the soiled paper towels in the trash and eyed herself critically in the mirror. At least now she didn't look like a dangerous fugitive who'd escaped a violent pack of leopard shifters who wanted her back alive or dead. Despite the warmth of the restroom, she shivered.

"Get back to the plan, Jackie," she told her mirrored self. She couldn't afford to fall apart, or everything she was afraid of would come to pass. She bent over to drink straight from the sink's faucet, then wiped the water off her face. She re-centered her her backpack and went out into the convenience store.

The smells of warm bread and sizzling hamburgers drew her like a lodestone toward the restaurant section, but she couldn't afford to waste the time or the money. She sternly made herself march into the back aisle and open the refrigerator door for the lunch meats and cheeses.

She got a whiff of a tantalizing scent as she pulled her

selections off the hooks. Not food, but something intensely interesting. Her sense of hearing and smell had magnified with each passing week of her pregnancy. She wished she knew if that was typical for a human woman carrying a shifter's child but she had no one to ask. Certainly not the lying son-of-a-bitch leopard who'd gotten her pregnant, despite her precautions. She hoped he was roasting in hell, but he probably wasn't. Justice for the privileged rich, regardless of skin color or species, had a whole different set of rules.

She let go of the refrigerator door and turned toward the scent, only to run headlong into a man who'd just turned down the aisle.

"Sorry," she said, even as he said the same word. She regained control of her suddenly clumsy feet. She got the impression of chiseled cheekbones and a square jaw before she dropped her gaze out of habit, one learned from living with volatile shifters. His scent hit her like a freight train a moment later, all woodsy and leathery and mouth-wateringly male.

No one, not even the father of her baby, back when she'd thought she was in love with him and he with her, had ever smelled that good. She took a step back, because if she hadn't, she'd have been tempted to stick her face in the vee of his short-sleeved T-shirt and lick.

"My fault," he said. "Are you..." He trailed off and audibly swallowed.

She made the mistake of looking up at him and confirmed that he was the sexiest man she'd ever seen, even counting the handsome actors she'd thrilled over as a teenager. His brown skin and features spoke of an ethnic heritage something like hers, and his warm, coppery-brown eyes threatened to drown her on the spot. His wide shoulders and arms looked strong enough to protect her from anything. The few tight coils of hair on his muscled chest mirrored the close-cropped hair on his head. His low-slung jeans and boots completed the mesmerizing package.

She swallowed and took another step back, away from temptation. "I'm fine."

Except she wasn't. She wanted to set fire to all her plans in favor of getting to know the man standing in front of her. For his part, he looked stunned.

She shook herself. Not, not, not happening. She was a pregnant fugitive with enough secrets to write her own soap opera, and an implacable enemy on her tail. A human, no matter how tall, broad-shouldered, and sexy, was no match for a criminal cat-shifter pride with claws and teeth, and vengeance on their minds.

She clutched her meat and cheese packages to her chest and turned away, even though her now throbbing body and aching breasts begged her to get closer. She'd learned to ride out the hormonal roller coaster of being pregnant, so she could damn well ride this out, too.

She made her way to the register, then realized she'd forgotten milk. Before she'd gotten pregnant, she'd been allergic to the stuff, and she still disliked it, but carrying a leopard-shifter's child made her crave it, so she compromised by drinking chocolate milk whenever she could.

She left her purchases on the counter, ignoring the blonde clerk's irritated look. Better that than having the woman accuse Jackie of shoplifting. Been there, done that, had the long wait for the cops.

She ignored her impulse to find Mr. Broad Shoulders again and walked to the other side of the store where the drink coolers took up a whole wall.

Two men who looked enough alike to be brothers were arguing in front of the beer case. They wore loose, motorcycle-club leather vests over their dusty jeans and T-shirts and stank of stale sweat and belched beer.

The taller man pulled the six-pack of yellow cans out of the shorter man's arms and shoved it back in the case. "No way am I drinking that swill." He grabbed a carton of brown bottles and shoved it into the other man's arms.

The shorter man shoved the carton back into the other's hands and grabbed the cans again. "I'm not pissing Dad off. You can fucking buy your own."

Jackie hesitated, then told herself just to get her milk and get out. She marched to the door, opened it, and grabbed the first chocolate milk carton she saw. Her baby picked that moment to kick hard and sharp. "Shouldn't have watched that kung fu movie last week," she muttered toward her belly.

"Hi, there, foxy lady. I'm Wiley."

She flinched in surprise. Somehow, the shorter man with the dark eyes and thin mouth had snuck up on her and was standing close enough to grab her.

"Your face'd be prettier if you'd smile." He was only a couple of inches taller than her five-foot-eight height. He scented the air like a dog. "Damn, woman. You smell fucking great." His eyes narrowed, and his focus intensified.

She backed away, fear rising. Only shifters noticed her scent like that. She couldn't help it that she smelled like a sexy baby factory to shifter males, even when she was pregnant. It was just her luck to run into shifters in an all-night truck stop. She'd had enough of the lazy, greedy breed to last a lifetime.

"Back off," she said firmly, dropping her arm so her helmet's strap slid down her forearm into her waiting hand.

The taller man came up behind Wiley. "How much for a BJ?"

It took her a moment to realize he thought she was a truck-stop prostitute. "Not for sale," she snapped. She'd take time to be outraged later.

She backed up another step, but Wiley grabbed her arm. The movement knocked the milk carton out of her hand. The carton bounced once and began leaking.

The taller man eyed her stomach and sneered. "Everything's for sale if the price is right. Fat girls like you oughta be grateful for what you can get."

Her jaw dropped. *Fat girl?*

The taller man weaved a little and reeked of alcohol. It took pounding down a lot of hard liquor for a shifter to get drunk. He scented the air, and his smile turned feral. "We'll show you a real good time."

Her fear and anger spiked. "I said no!" She stomped hard on Wiley's instep, then kneed him.

He buckled in pain. Not even shifters were immune to nut shots.

She pivoted and ran toward the bathrooms where she'd noticed a back door. Adrenaline gave her feet wings.

She heard curses behind her as she rounded the corner into the hallway. She hit the door's exit bar at top speed and burst through it into the wide alley. The buildings cast darker shadows at dusk. She stumbled as she lost traction on the dirt and gravel, but recovered and took off to the left, away from the multiple trash bins and toward the well-lit asphalt parking lot. Maybe she could get help from some of the truckers.

She'd almost made it to the pavement when she heard pounding footsteps and growling behind her. Acting on instinct, she veered right, then used her momentum to spin around. She bashed the tall, drunk man on the head with her helmet.

He staggered and fell to one knee. "Fuck!"

She launched into a run, only to get jerked back when he grabbed the back hem of her jacket. She spun sideways, out of his grasp, and swung at him again with the helmet.

He blocked it with his forearm, then ripped the helmet from her grasp and threw it away.

She backed up.

He clambered to his feet and smiled. "Feisty! I like that." He reached out long arms to corral her, but she dodged away.

She fumbled in the pocket of her cargo jeans and pulled out the slender, rusty pipe, then powered it.

From the back doorway, a big dog—no, a coyote burst out and landed. It trotted straight for her. The coyote was larger than its animal-world counterpart, as some shifters were.

The tall man grabbed for her again.

"No!" She thwacked his exposed wrist with her pipe. A blue spark flashed. He jerked back and howled in pain. She jabbed the pipe into his stomach.

He fell sideways and spasmed like he'd been hit with a cattle prod. Which he had, after a fashion, because that's what the magic she'd stored in the tube did.

The coyote slowed and stalked toward her, growling with yellow-eyed menace.

She took a swipe at his muzzle with her tube. "Back off, fur butt!"

She felt something on her leg and looked down just as the tall man's hand clamped around her ankle. He growled through temporarily distorted teeth. Shit, he was changing right there, in almost-public, without bothering to take off his clothes. The first coyote lunged forward to grab her forearm. She shrieked, but her husky voice had never been very loud. She pushed her forearm into his mouth to make him gag and back off, grimly hanging onto her pipe.

A huge, rounded shadow emerged from the other end of the alley, near the trash bins. It barreled toward them with a roar loud enough to reverberate off the brick walls.

The coyote spun to face the new menace with a snarl.

The taller man finished shifting and shook off the shreds of his pants and ripped vest. The remnants of his T-shirt looked like a cheap collar.

She backed away, intending to run, but found herself unable to take her eyes off the largest, shaggiest bear she'd ever seen. Not that she'd seen one up close before. It was as big as a diesel pickup truck and had distinctive pale markings across its furry nose and chest.

The first coyote darted sideways to slash sharp teeth at the bear's throat. The bear ignored him as it swung a mighty paw at the T-shirt coyote, knocking him back a good ten feet. T-shirt coyote slowly scrabbled to his feet, shaking his head as if dazed.

The other coyote danced back, and then in again, biting the bear's shoulder. The bear turned and snapped wickedly long teeth at the coyote. He nimbly dodged away.

The T-shirt coyote lunged forward and bit at the bear's other shoulder, but only came away with a mouthful of shaggy fur. The bear growled and swatted the T-shirt coyote again. This time, he flew through the air and hit the brick wall of the store hard with a pained yip, then fell to the ground.

The bear turned to snap at the other coyote again. The coyote scrambled backward, then lunged in and bit the bear's flank.

The bear sat on him.

The squashed coyote whined, then was silent.

She glanced at the T-shirt coyote, but he lay unmoving in the dirt.

A powerful wave of something indescribable buffeted her senses, sort of like magic, but not. It seemed to come from the bear, and felt like an imperative to do something, but she didn't know what.

Her brain managed to get a coherent thought past her shock. If the huge bear shifter with equally huge claws thought she smelled really good, she'd have no chance at all of getting away. Fear galvanized her into backing up with tiny, shuffling steps. Maybe he wouldn't notice...

The bear whined, and she froze.

The massive animal heaved itself up and forward. Even as she watched, the flattened coyote was shifting back into a naked man. He was out cold. A quick glance toward the wall told her the other shifter was now human, too, wearing nothing but the ragged T-shirt collar.

The bear took a step toward her.

She trembled with the need to run but running prey excited predator shifters. She couldn't help the whimper of fear that escaped her.

More not-magic brushed her senses, this time like a velvety soft blanket against her skin.

In an instant, the bear became a fully clothed man wearing jeans and a V-necked T-shirt over a hundred yards of muscles. Mr. Broad Shoulders himself.

Of course, the hottest man on Earth would turn out to be a shifter.

"Are you hurt?" His tone matched his worried expression. Even his voice made her want to step closer so he could whisper in her ear.

"No, I'm fine." Her baby took that moment to kick, and she winced.

He took one small step forward. "You're in pain."

"It'll go away." She darted her gaze away for a moment to look for her helmet. "Thank you for helping me." She kept her eyes on him as she took a trial step away, to see how he reacted. When he did nothing but stand there, with worry tightening his wide, kissable mouth, she moved slowly toward her helmet, watching him the whole time. Her makeshift magic-powered pipe needed recharging, so she slid it into the pocket of her cargo pants before bending over to pick up the helmet.

He cleared his throat. "Could I, er, buy you a cup of coffee?" His tone almost sounded shy.

Yes, yes, yes, sang her body, suddenly flush with raging hormones. She almost swayed toward him.

No, no, no, shouted her rational brain, the one that had plans. The first and only time she'd listened to her body, she'd ended up pregnant and an unwilling captive of a feline-shifter pride.

"Thanks, but I'm already running late." She sidled toward the asphalt edge of the parking lot. It felt wrong to move away from him, but her situation made anything between them impossible. "I'm truly grateful for what you did." She tilted her head toward the men lying in the alley. "Shifting in public like that means they're fur-brained fatheads. Neither of us should be here when they wake up."

"Let me at least walk you to wherever your bike is parked." He pointed a thumb toward the convenience store's back door. "They may have buddies."

She hesitated, then sighed. "Okay. Thanks." She should have thought of that. Asshole shifters always had buddies.

She stepped up onto the asphalt. He put his hands in his

pockets and rounded his shoulders, as if trying to make himself look harmless. He failed miserably, because it drew attention to his low-slung jeans and made her wonder what he'd look like without them. She'd bet her motorcycle he'd look a damn sight better than two scrawny coyotes.

They walked quietly together as the parking lot's lights blinked on. His mother must have brought him up right, because he matched his stride to hers and kept a respectful distance. She allowed herself the secret, impossible fantasy that he was her man and she was his woman.

"Do you have someone you can call?" He glanced at her stomach, then away. "A mate, maybe?"

"No, thank God. I've had quite enough of shifters for a while." Realizing what she'd said, she added hastily, "Present company excepted."

He shrugged one shoulder, but his mouth twitched with humor. It gave her the wild impulse to do whatever it took to see him really smile, because she just knew he'd be stunning. And she shouldn't be having those thoughts. She was a total basket case.

The sun dipped to touch the highest mountains to the west just as they arrived at her motorcycle. It looked lonely, standing by itself.

She shook off the fantasy, then looked up into his beautiful coppery eyes. "Thank you again."

"I was thinking." He tightened his hands into fists in his pockets, making his arm muscles bulge. "My semi only has half a load in the trailer. I could put your bike in there and take you someplace safe for the night."

She shook her head. "That's a gracious offer, but I need to keep moving." She zipped up the jacket to prevent it from flapping in the wind and turned the kerchief at her neck around, so she could pull it up over her mouth to protect against road dust.

His eyes darkened. "If you're in trouble, maybe I can help."

He was making this so hard. "If I were in trouble, it would be horribly unfair of me to drag you into it, after you kicked coyote-shifter ass for me." She fished the key out of her pocket and put it in the ignition.

"I wouldn't mind." His resolute expression hinted at stubborn determination. He glanced to her stomach again. "You shouldn't be unprotected."

She appreciated his tact. He'd obviously figured out she was pregnant. Shifters could scent that kind of thing immediately. The coyotes should have noticed, but they'd been too drunk on high-test booze and shifter-mate lust.

"I shouldn't be a lot of things, but here I am." An absurd thought crossed her mind, and her eyes went wide. "Oh my God! The name of the shifter you sat on was Wiley. You sat on Wiley Coyote!" She almost doubled over with laughter. It felt like forever since she'd found anything to laugh about.

His wide grin was every bit as sexy as the rest of him. "He must hate those cartoons."

Still chuckling, she undid the helmet's strap. "I'll remember seeing that for the rest of my life." She hoped he'd think she meant his bear form sitting on the coyote, and not his amazing smile that would be etched in her memory forever.

She dusted off the faceplate on her pants, relieved to find it not even scratched. She pulled the helmet on and secured the strap under her chin.

He pulled his wallet out and handed her a card. "This is me. That number is for a cellular phone that's in my rig. If you ever need me to sit on someone, or you just want to talk, I hope you'll call me."

She took the card and read the top line out loud. "Trevor Hammond Independent Trucking." She put the card safely in the zippered pocket over her chest. "I'm Jackie Breton, by the way. Well, Jacqueline, but only my mother and my former boss called me that." That was another life, one she could never go back to. She pulled out her gloves and put them on.

"Nice to meet you, Jackie." He stepped back. He looked as deeply unhappy as she felt, but that didn't make much sense. He was a big, strong, healthy bear shifter, with wicked-long claws and magic, not an almost powerless, pregnant, terrified human on the run.

She straddled her bike and rocked it forward, letting the motion close the kickstand. She started the engine, gunned the hand throttle enough to make a slow circle, then straightened out and headed for the parking lot's exit. She briefly lifted one hand and waved in case Trevor was still watching.

She liked the sound of his name. Hell, she liked the sound of everything about him, not to mention wanting to rub herself over every inch of him, even though she hadn't been force-changed into a feline. If her life ever got normal again, maybe she would call him.

She shook her head. Her life was not Last of the Mohicans, with her handsome savior telling her to stay alive and promising that no matter where she went, he would find her. It was more like Marked for Death, where she'd be lucky to survive the vindictive people after her.

She squared her shoulders and got back to her plan. It was her best shot at staying alive. Probably her only shot.

2

Trevor Hammond didn't think of himself as a violent man, but at that moment, with the woman his bear insisted was his true mate leaving him in a dwindling dust cloud, he wanted to go back behind the store and kick more drunk-coyote ass.

He could not have screwed up the first meeting with his mate any more if he'd tried. If he was honest, he had to admit he'd doubted he'd ever find a mate, considering his bear was one of a kind. Aunt Straya, who had raised him, had always told him to trust in the moon goddess, and be ready, but who would ever expect to run into his entirely human mate in an all-night truck stop known for its shifter customers?

He'd tracked a tantalizing smell and almost bowled her over with his carelessness. Then her overwhelmingly nuanced and fascinating scent had lit up every cell in his body. Mate, his bear had growled, then ordered him to lick her and claim her right there in the lunch-meat aisle. His human side pointed out she was likely already mated, since she was pregnant and carrying the daughter of some sort of feline shifter. His bear countered that she didn't have a mate bond or smell mated, and no shifter would willingly leave his pregnant mate unprotected. And while he was arguing with himself, and hadn't even gotten out a coherent sentence, the tall, diffident woman had left him.

And to top it off, instead of going after her, he'd retreated to the back alley to get control of himself and come up with an approach that wouldn't scare the life out of her. Because the second and third things he'd finally noticed were the sour taste of her fear and the submissive body language. Someone had conditioned his proud, strong, stunningly beautiful mate into outward displays of obeisance. He'd paced off his anger in the alley behind the dumpsters while racking his brain for something better to say to her than "Wanna see my truck?"

To his shame, he hadn't immediately noticed that the problem in the alley involved her. Shifters often went out back to scuffle. Otto, the owner, fined or banned anyone who disturbed the peace inside, and no one wanted to be gored or stomped by an oversized, pissed-off Texas-longhorn bull shifter.

All it took was for a woman's voice to shout "No" for his bear to take control and shift. Thank the goddess his magic took care of his clothes. His bear had recognized what his human part should have, the presence of his mate. He bounded toward the trouble in time to see her use a magic weapon on the attacker, and another coyote joining the attack.

He roared his rage and brought the fight to them. Two drunks were no match for a mad bear defending his mate. They were lucky he hadn't maimed or killed them. He'd managed to gain enough control to warn his bear that the deaths would scare his mate even more than she already was. And then he'd had to let her ride off on her motorcycle alone, or he'd be as bad as the mangy coyotes.

The only good things that came out of their first meeting were that he now knew her name, he'd found out she really was unmated despite being pregnant with a shifter baby, and she'd taken his card.

But he could feel in the depths of his soul, through the potential connection already forming between them, she was in deadly trouble and needed his help. Which she wouldn't take, because she didn't know or trust him, and she deeply disliked shifters.

He couldn't say he was fond of them, either, at that moment. Humans with shifter-mate potential were meant to be wooed and cherished, since they helped ensure the longevity and genetic diversity of all shifter species, even whatever kind of bear his was. Jackie was so much more than the door prize for lame-ass wolf wannabes, or the catnip play toy of whatever lowlife feline had gotten her pregnant and abandoned her.

He went back into the truck stop long enough to warn them about the naked numbskulls out back and buy extra food, then he climbed into the cab of his rig and pulled out his Nebraska maps. He'd worked long hours to pay off the bank loan on his truck six months before. And since it also served as his home, he'd been using his more recent profits to trick it out with improvements and creature comforts.

The best investment had been the built-in cellular phone, which paid for itself in making him much faster at responding to hauling opportunities and notifying shippers about delays. Rural coverage was nonexistent, but big cities were putting up cell towers every day. Now he was doubly thankful, because it was his only mundane-world connection to Jackie.

He didn't know how to use his spotty magic to tell him anything about her, other than it felt like she was headed due east, probably on Interstate 80 toward Nebraska. Now he wished he'd practiced with his magic more diligently, like his aunt had nagged him about, instead of only using it for small tricks to win bar bets.

His half-load was furniture, and wasn't due for three days, but it was bad for business to drive due east when his destination was supposed to be north. He figured he could be one day late, but then he'd have to give up the load to someone else. There would always be another load, but there might never be another mate.

He drove to the I-80 entrance ramp and headed toward Nebraska. Night fell fast once he got beyond the city lights of Cheyenne, and past the stench of the refineries east of town. He had no idea how humans tolerated it, except that in Wyoming, oil was gold.

Every motorcycle he saw made his bear surge forward, but the rider was never the brown jacket and flaming-skull helmet he was looking for. He wished he'd asked where she was going. Motorcycles traveled faster than his truck but took a lot more active attention. Truckers drove long hours, but bikers fatigued more quickly. He hadn't missed the faint shadows under her beautiful brown eyes.

He usually listened to music while he drove, but he was too worried about Jackie, and too worried about horrible possibilities. For the first time in his thirty-six years, he had something to lose that meant more to him than anything, and it terrified him. Maybe she and the father of her baby hadn't parted willingly, and he was searching for her to claim her as his mate. Maybe whatever she was running from was more than one bear could handle. Maybe he'd make a rotten mate because he was so very young compared to other shifters, who lived centuries. Maybe she'd never get over her prejudice against shifters.

The ringing of his cellular phone nearly made him leap out of his seat. He reduced his speed and pulled into the right lane, then answered the call using the hands-free speakers he and an electrician friend had rigged.

"Trevor, what are you doing?"

"Aunt Straya? Are you okay?" She disliked phones in general, and only used them for emergencies.

"That's what I called to ask you." Cellular phones were a modern miracle, but they made everyone sound like they were in the bottom of a well. *"Auris came pounding on my door, wailing about signs and portents. I thought she'd been sampling the fairy moondew again, but she's sober as a judge."* No one knew what Auris was running from, and she was more than a bit of a drama queen, but his aunt didn't discriminate against the lost and unwanted who found their way into her woods.

"What did she say?" asked Trevor.

"That you and your mate need to find sanctuary before the full moon, or your blood will paint the canyons. What's this about a mate, and why do I have to hear it from Auris?" To his aunt, the news about a mate would be much more important than the threat on his life.

He suppressed a frustrated noise. "It's complicated." He told her about the disastrous first meeting and what little he knew.

"You always did pick the hardest path up the mountain." Trevor rolled his eyes. He preferred peace and quiet, but the fates seemed to have other plans for him. *"Best you get yourself and your woman to Kotoyeesinay as soon as you can.*

Ask for sanctuary the moment you cross the glade's border. The elves will hear you."

"I will."

"*Bring her here, afterward. I want to meet the woman who has your measure.*"

Trevor gave an audible growl. "I will not. You'll show her your photo album, and she'll laugh at me the rest of my life."

"*You need laughter. Drive safe.*" As usual, when his aunt was done talking, she simply hung up.

Kotoyeesinay was west, behind him, high in the Rocky Mountains near the Wyoming border with Colorado. He'd been there several times, but not for a few years. He remembered the sharply winding canyon road that seemed to take far longer than it should for the distance shown on the map. Elven glade magic, he guessed.

The call he'd been hoping for came through thirty minutes later, though not the way he expected.

"Is this Mr. Hammond?" an older man's voice queried.

"Yes." Dispatchers didn't usually call at nine-thirty at night.

"The wife and I have a young lady here at the house. She took a bad tumble on her motorbike. Won't let me call the police or an ambulance, but she said I could call you."

Trevor dawdled in closing up the back of his trailer, to make sure the old rancher made it safely down the driveway to his front yard. Only the moon lit the landscape, and humans didn't have good night vision. Trevor pretended he needed the man's help lifting the bike into the trailer, because while he could have done it easily, it was too heavy for a normal man, even one of Trevor's human size and build.

He climbed into the cab and shut the door, then slid the saddlebags he'd taken off her bike into the storage area behind her seat. "How are you holding up?"

He'd bundled her into the passenger seat first, as carefully as he could. The whole left side of her was one big bruise, and her knee had swollen to twice its normal size.

He'd parked on the farm road where she'd dumped her bike and gotten pinned under it. She'd been lucky the rancher found her. It was probably bad of Trevor to enjoy carrying her from the rancher's house to his truck. His anxious, angry bear was easier to soothe when taking in her scent with every breath.

Jackie gave him a crooked smile. "I've had better days."

"I'll bet." He wanted to take her to the nearest hospital. His bear wanted to take her to a cave and protect her while she healed. "What do you want to do?"

"Is my motorcycle drivable?"

"I don't know much about bikes." Inspired, he added, "But I know someone who does. He lives in a small town called Kotoyeesinay, in south Wyoming." Trevor was pretty sure Shepherd, some type of ogre mix, and seven feet tall, would still be there. He didn't fit in with the outside modern world very well.

She shook her head. "That's the wrong direction. I need to get to Chicago."

He waited to see if she'd explain, but she didn't. "By when?"

"Today. Yesterday." She moved her leg and winced. "Do you know how to get in touch with the Shifter Tribunal?"

That was the last question he'd expected. "No, sorry." Her trouble must be worse than he'd thought. "I could make some calls. A couple of my customers are big packs and prides—"

"No," she said, cutting him off. "No shifters."

That stung a little. A lot, actually.

"I'm sorry," she said in a low, breathy tone. "That was incredibly rude." She looked away, toward the moonlit field of half-grown corn to her right. "You've been nothing but kind to me, and I'm lashing out at you because of my shitty choices." She sniffled and wiped at her face. "I'm the last person to hate someone for the color of their, uh, fur. Had enough of that growing up in Weirtree, where they still resent losing the Civil War and think magic is the devil's work. It's just that outside of you, my experiences with actual shifters haven't been good."

He desperately wanted to hear her story, comfort her, make things better for her, but they couldn't stay parked on a deserted farm road in the Nebraska hinterland. "We should get moving, or your rescuer will be back out here with questions." He started the engine. "I could take you to a motel."

Her head snapped around to give him a wide-eyed look. He added hastily, "I can sleep here in the truck, but you need a real bed."

The tension in her expression eased, and she put her hand over her rounded stomach. "And a real bathroom." She snorted. "I think I've used every damn one of them between here and Pagosa Springs."

"That's in southern Colorado, isn't it? Near the mountains?" He inched the truck forward until he was sure the wheels were on the road before accelerating. He didn't know what else to do but just drive. All the way to Chicago, if that's what it took.

She was silent for long moments. "If I tell you what's

going on..." She trailed off, then started again. "I just met you, but I already know you'll want to help, and I want to let you, because you're the first person who's made me feel safe in the last six months. Longer than that, actually. Which is crazy, but it's true." She blew out a loud breath. "But it's a fucking mess and could get you hurt or killed."

He tightened his hands on the steering wheel to help control the part of him that wanted to make a threat display at whoever made her sound so disconsolate. "Tell you what. You tell me the situation, and I promise not to go off half-cocked or get us in worse trouble. Deal?"

Out of the corner of his eye, he saw her cast a couple of sidelong glances at him. "It's weird that you know what I'm thinking." She used her hands to lift her sore leg, wincing as she did. "Or maybe not weird. Are you using your magic on me? I felt it, in the alley, but I couldn't tell what it was doing. I've only been around witches and fairies."

"No," he said. "Most of my magic is bound up in my shifting. Maybe you felt when I commanded the coyotes to shift to human?" He shrugged one shoulder. "That's an alpha thing." He felt guilty for not mentioning the gossamer-thin mate bond between them, which was already giving him hints, but he had the feeling she wasn't ready for that part. He wasn't sure he was, either. Not if the woman his bear wanted to claim couldn't get over her hate for shifters.

"I didn't know shifters had free magic. I thought it was all for shifting." Her tone blended curiosity with caution.

"It's uncommon. Mine isn't much." He pointed to a wide shoulder on the road, meant for slow farm vehicles to pull over to let traffic pass. "We could stop there for a bit."

She nodded, so he slowed the truck to a stop and turned off the engine. If it got too cool for her, he could turn on a heater.

The moonlight lent her beautiful face exotic mystery. Her complex scent filled his senses and sent desire thrumming through his veins and blood toward his dick. He sternly told himself to stand down, or he'd be no better than the drunken coyotes.

"I work... used to work for a Houston accounting firm. One of my coworkers is... was part fairy and thinks all magical people should be friends. She introduced me to a rich real estate developer named Barry Wills. My mom told me about shifters, so I knew they existed, but he was the first one I actually met. He's a spotted leopard. He liked me right away and let me know it. Romantic gifts, glitzy parties, gala openings. I fell for him hard. He found me so unbelievably sexy, even in a room full of much richer, prettier women."

Trevor only barely managed to repress a growl from his bear, who didn't like Jackie thinking of herself as anything less than stop-traffic gorgeous. He also didn't like the thought that a sneaky leopard had been in her bed, but he couldn't say he'd been celibate all his life, either.

"Barry said I was his mate, but whenever I wanted him to go with me to visit my mother in east Texas, or I asked about his family or pride, he'd tell me it was worse than a soap opera and change the subject or avoid me for a few days." She shook her head. "My boss sent me and a couple of coworkers to a CPA conference in Las Vegas in February as a reward for our hard work. Barry came with me because he loves the nightlife."

She rubbed the top of her thigh a couple of times. "Now we get to the part where I only know some of what happened. The first night, Barry's condom broke, and I didn't think anything of it because I was on the pill. I wasn't going to raise a child alone like my widowed mother had to, and Barry was allergic to any talk about marriage. He said only humans cared about that. The second night, we had a fight, and Barry went partying without me. The third night, he prepared a romantic bubble bath for us in the spa tub with two-hundred-dollar-an-ounce perfume and vintage champagne and told me he was sorry. Afterward, I was sleepy, so he carried me to the bed." The breath she blew out almost sounded like hissing. She looked away, then met his eyes again. "The next thing I remember, someone was slapping me awake. I was buck naked in an old, tiny windowless room that smelled like stale cigarette smoke."

He couldn't help the growl that rumbled in his chest. He clenched his hands together.

She gave him a sour look. "Save your growls, cowboy, 'cause it don't get any better from here." She crossed her arms over her breasts. "It was an illegal auction house in the basement of an older casino. Seems I have 'shifter-mate potential,' which makes shifters of any species drunk with lust and want to have babies with me. Thank heavens it repulses vampires. The auction house put me up for sale within hours because they knew something I didn't: I was pregnant. The lion shifter who bought me for his pride should have noticed, too, but I still smelled like knock-out drugs and perfume. Roehm—who turned out to be the pride's leader—spent all his time feeling up the younger girls he bought instead of inspecting the women."

Trevor cursed. "Where exactly is this casino?"

Her expression turned wary. "What will you do if I tell you?"

Remembering his promise not to go off half-cocked, he took in a deep breath and let it out slowly. "Sorry. I've heard rumors of an auction, but I didn't believe it." He let his determination show on his face. "I do now."

"I was only there for a day, but I saw males and females

of half a dozen species chained on the auction block. Right out of that Roots mini-series. Most of the 'shifter-mate potential' group were like me, kidnapped and clueless. Our bidders were shifter outfits. I could smell the odor of corruption, even through the gazillion suppression and concealment spells all over." She shuddered. "Roehm bought six of us. The auction house shot us with tranq darts, and we woke up in a former motel complex outside Pagosa Springs. It's in southern Colorado like you thought."

"Lion pride?" he asked.

"Mixed, and males only. Roehm's a mean-looking white guy and an African lion. Claims he's five hundred years old, but he doesn't know shit about history, so I think he's much younger. The two lazy-ass litter mates who paid Roehm for me—Ricardo and his brother Ruben—are regular leopards. The pride has three more leopards, a jaguar, a tiger, a cheetah, four lynxes, and eight mountain lions. Something wrong with every damn one of them."

He tilted his head. "Wrong?"

"Crippled, feral, addicted, weak, fat, you name it. The lynxes are orphaned litter mates, barely out of the den, and don't know any better. I can't prove it, but I think Roehm murdered the old pride leader, then drove off or killed anyone he couldn't dominate. He's the one-eyed king in the land of the blind."

"What did they do when they discovered you were pregnant?" He knew he wouldn't like the answer but needed to hear it.

"Slapped me around like it was my fault. Yelled a lot. Tried to get their money back, but the contract said the 'livestock' was sold 'as is.'" She snorted. "Who'd have thought illegal auction houses selling creatures of myth and magic would use mundane contracts?"

Trevor nodded. "Signed in blood, I'll bet. Makes it easier to exact magical penalties."

"That makes sense. The staff were all wizards and sorcerers. Anyway, Ricardo and Ruben couldn't stand to be around me because I smelled like vomit from non-stop morning sickness, and because I carried another leopard's child. Ricardo boasted about being civilized because they planned to sell the baby to the auction house. Before Roehm took over, the former leader made the pride abandon any non-pride cubs in the high mountains."

Trevor passed beyond shock and into dangerously angry territory. Shifter offspring were not accidents or commodities. His bear roared in his head. Someday, he promised himself, there would be a reckoning. He took two deep, long breaths and blew them out slowly to rein in his temper. "Go on."

"Since I had to live in their pigsty of a mobile home, I spent the first two weeks cleaning it, because the stench made my morning sickness even worse. My mother cleans people's houses for a living, and I used to help her." She jutted out her chin in an unspoken challenge, as if daring him to judge her.

He'd had a similar chip on his shoulder growing up. "My aunt takes in laundry and sells put-up vegetables from her garden that the county food inspectors didn't know about." He crooked a corner of his mouth. "When I was a wild and restless teenager, looking for trouble, she had me shift and use my big claws to rototill her garden and chase off the nocturnal pest animals at night."

She looked startled, then returned his smile. "Smart woman." She shook her head. "Roehm sends the pride out to sell illegal drugs and guns, and steal cars, but Ricardo is obese and lazy, and Ruben is skinny and lazy. I gave them the idea to sell my cleaning services to the other pride members." She wrinkled her nose. "You'd think shifters couldn't stand eye-watering smells from filth. And don't get me started on their personal hygiene. Anywhere outside is their cat box."

It took him a minute to realize why she'd volunteered to be the maid. "You became invisible. No one notices the help."

She waved her hand. "I didn't think of that at first. I just wanted information, like where the hell the compound was, and how soon could I escape." She shivered. "Luckily, I've always been an over-planner, or I'd have been eaten by the near-feral tiger guard that Roehm keeps chained at night or burned to ash by the magical wards they paid a wizard to install on their perimeter, or beaten to death for trying to steal one of the pride's cars." She shuddered. "Or dead from a failed forced change like poor Dale."

Trevor was so wrapped up in Jackie's story that he almost missed the far-off glint of headlights at the intersection about a mile in front of them. He used his alpha magic to borrow night vision from his bear. He pointed out the windshield. "Pickup truck with two men in it. Two shotguns in the rack behind their heads."

"Maybe we should find that motel you mentioned." She made a wry face. "Or at least a public bathroom."

He started the engine and turned on the headlights. "There's a file box under your seat. The map of Nebraska is on top. Use the flashlight and see where you want to go. I mark motels with a letter 'M' if they're decent."

He pulled onto the road just as the pickup truck passed them, taking care to keep his face and hands in shadow. Jackie's story had him wanting to avoid creating the memorable sight of a black man and woman in a big-rig truck in the middle of Nebraska farm country at night. "I'll turn south at the intersection. We're about eight miles from the interstate."

"Do you mind if I use magic on your map to find someplace safe?"

He didn't blame her for the caution in her voice. Magic could be a touchy subject, even among people who knew it was real. "Sure, if it's not destructive. Good maps are hard to replace."

The power overspill caressed him like an ocean wave, hardening him to an erection and making his body sing. He wished he had something to put over his lap. Not even diving naked into an icy pond would help at this point.

Out of the corner of his eye, he saw her spread out the map. She waved her hand, and points on the map appeared like tiny sparkles.

He slowed for the intersection, glancing at the map. "What's that bright blue spot?"

She lifted the map and pointed the flashlight at it. "Ko-something or another, in Wyoming." She frowned. "What was the name of the town your mechanic friend lives in?"

"Kotoyeesinay." He should tell her about the call from his aunt.

"That's the place." She made a frustrated sound. "Damnit. As of this moment, that's the only safe place to be in the four-state span of this map." She dropped it to her lap. "But I'll be backtracking instead of adding distance between me and the pride's hunters and enforcers. Regardless, we can't make it there tonight."

The exhaustion in her voice concerned him. "How about the closest safe motel, for now? You can do the map spell again after you've had a few hours' rest."

He kept his eyes forward, toward the intersection, but

everything else in him focused on her. She had to be close to her breaking point and could still kick his shifter ass out of her life. He didn't know what he would do if she did.

"Okay. Turn right. The Lark Sleepytime Inn is about six miles south on the left."

He let out the breath he'd been holding and turned right.

3

Jackie woke to sunrise and snoring. It took a few seconds for her brain to boot up and remember where she was and why she was so comfortable. She opened her eyes and looked to the floor where a larger-than-life, short-snouted, curiously long-haired bear slept stretched out in front of the motel room's door, gently snoring. She smiled. He'd be one hell of a surprise for any intruders.

After renting the room for her, Trevor the man had carried her from the truck into the room. He'd made it seem easy, even though she was taller than average and nowhere close to skinny. She'd loved the feel of his strength, the sound of his steady heartbeat in her ear as she rested her head on his chest.

She'd invited him to sleep in the room with the idea of sharing the queen-sized bed, instead of making him sleep in his truck. She'd joked that his honor was safe with her, but it might not have been. Despite her injuries from the accident, despite being pregnant, and despite having just met him, her body burned for him. Her breasts ached for the touch of his calloused hands, the soft wetness of his mouth. She wanted him surrounding her, holding her, inside her. Her core pulsed at the thought.

Then her stupid bladder spasmed, and she'd had to limp to the bathroom to answer the call of nature. The mirror's reflection of her scraped and filthy self told her she was in no shape to seduce anyone.

While she was in the shower, Trevor had brought in packaged sandwiches and chips from the cooler in his truck and written her a note suggesting she treat her knee with the ice he got from the machine outside the motel's office. He couldn't tell her about it because he'd shifted into his bear form and dozed near the front door.

Maybe it was for the best, since sex would only complicate their situation. From little looks and touches, and the unmistakable bulge in his jeans, she knew he wanted her as much as she wanted him. But she was bloated and fat, so his attraction was probably the shifter-mate potential thing. She'd never been the type of woman who drew men like bears to honey. She'd drifted off to sleep after her feeble joke.

The bedside clock now said it was a few minutes before six. She sat up cautiously, but her soreness had vanished in the night. Her knee still twinged, but she knew it would be fine in a few more hours. One of the pluses of carrying a shifter's baby was she apparently benefited from the speedy shifter healing. The improved sense of taste and smell had made her morning sickness worse, but the better hearing and reflexes had helped her survive in a compound full of frustrated, quick-with-a-fist shifters. Roehm had assumed that by forbidding Ricardo and Ruben to force-change her into a leopard while she was pregnant, she'd be weak and powerless.

Enough of the past, she told herself. The day beckoned... and so did the bathroom.

By the time she returned from brushing her teeth and twisting and smoothing her hair into something resembling civilized, Trevor had shifted back to human.

The vee of his T-shirt drew her eyes to his deliciously broad and muscular chest. "Does your magic let you keep your clothes?" Would he taste as good as he smelled? Would his nipples be wide and sensitive to the touch of her tongue? She gave herself an internal shake. Timing, girl, timing.

"Yes. My aunt taught me. Magic runs in our family. I trained myself to shift really fast, so I could go more places I wasn't supposed to and not get caught."

She raised her eyebrows. "Wasn't a big, woolly bear kind of noticeable?"

He smiled ruefully. "And now you see the flaw in my teenage logic."

She rolled up the sleeves of her faded denim shirt. It wouldn't fit over her belly much longer. "I was always the straight-laced, straight-A student, but it didn't help. All most people saw was the mixed-race daughter of a witchy white woman who scandalously married a black man, who got himself killed fixing an electrical tower." She sighed. "Now I wish I'd done some of the wild things in all those rumors."

His smile gentled. "Smart gets you farther than wild."

Tears threatened, and his face showed worry. "Don't mind me." She waved him away. "You're a good listener, and I'm on the pregnancy-hormone rollercoaster. It's a crying jag one moment, and a craving for banana Moon pies the next." She rolled her eyes and pointed to her belly. "And nasty chocolate milk for Junior."

The concern didn't leave his face. "You need breakfast."

She wiped away the tear that fell. She couldn't

remember the last time anyone had been so considerate of her. "Yeah so do you, but let's check the map first."

He spread it out on the dresser. The night before, she'd made it into a magic talisman that showed safety in blue and threats in red, and the safest route away from danger. All they had to do was wave a hand over it to make the pinpoints light up again. She shook her head dubiously. "Kotoyeesinay is still blue but look at the red swarm coming up from Denver. If we make it to Laramie and the mountains ahead of them, we'll be boxed in by the mountains, with only the canyon road in front of us."

His eyes narrowed as he considered the map. "The motel has a big, fenced lot out back for storing RVs. If I pay them to store the trailer for a few days, my truck can go fast, even up canyon roads. I have more emergency food in my cooler. Not as good as a hot meal, but we won't starve."

The temptation to go with him rocked her, but that was pure selfishness. "You have a business to run. People who depend on you. A girlfriend. I can't ask you to just upend your life and take me to a small town in Wyoming."

"I'm not mated. It's just me and my truck, and I'm offering. And Kotoyeesinay is more than just a bright blue dot." He pointed to the map. "It's a sanctuary town."

"What's that?" She'd only heard of sanctuary cities in California that pledged not to hassle non-citizen migrants who'd been in the country for decades.

"They're each different. The US has three, and there's one in Canada and maybe one in Mexico. More around the world, I'm told. Kotoyeesinay was founded a couple of centuries ago by a refugee group of very powerful elves, and others have joined since. They take in peaceable folk who need a safe place to live, away from the human world, or the world of their kind. If they grant you sanctuary, their defenses are formidable."

She shook her head. "The only thing Roehm is afraid of is the Shifter Tribunal. Otherwise, he'll just keep coming, hurting more people because of me." She hooked her thumbs into the belt loops of her cheap maternity jeans to keep from touching him. "Hurting you."

He shook his head and crossed his arms. "My Aunt Straya takes in lost people. Gives them a place to heal, and time to figure out what they want to do. One of her rescues made my aunt call and tell me that I and my... that you and I need to be in sanctuary by the full moon. That's tomorrow night."

"What if we aren't?"

"Auris didn't say, but it's always been calamitous. She might be part death banshee."

Jackie suppressed a sigh. Anyone in the magical world could tell when they were being pushed around by one of the many hidden higher powers. It wasn't wise to thwart them.

"All right, but on two conditions." She stepped back and caught his eye, so he'd know she was serious. "One." She held up a finger. "If the town refuses me sanctuary, you won't argue with them. They have to protect their own."

He nodded, but unhappily.

"Two." She held up a second finger. "You have to promise you won't do something stupid and get yourself killed."

A flurry of emotions crossed his face as his jaw tightened. He nodded once.

She shook her head. "You have to say it. 'I promise not to do something stupid and get myself fucking killed.'"

He frowned deeply and bit out the words, then added, "Or you, either."

"Thank you." Tears welled up again, but she blinked until they went away, or she'd be crying all morning. "You probably won't believe me, but you're already the best friend I've ever had. I don't want to lose you."

"I do believe you." He reached out toward her, then hesitated. "Can I hold you?"

She closed the distance between them and wrapped her arms around his waist. His arms snuggled her into place, and she felt like she'd found home. Time stopped, then started again as her body woke up.

She nuzzled the side of her face into his chest and inhaled the sensual scent of bear and man. Angled as she was to accommodate her stomach, she couldn't help but feel his erection. Her nipples tightened in response as she heated with desire.

He groaned and tilted his head down just as she lifted hers. Their mouths and tongues met in eager exploration. He trailed kisses toward her ear and down her neck, and she could only gasp and push her chest into his to relieve the ache in her rock-hard nipples. She found his hand and moved it from her waist to her breast to tell him what she wanted. He drew another gasp from her as he rubbed a thumb across her breast. She grabbed handfuls of his muscular butt and pulled his pelvis toward hers. He rumbled throatily in response.

A car door slam and a shout from the parking lot woke her from the delicious but dangerous haze. "Trevor..."

He was already loosening his arms. "We should get going." He stepped back, but not before giving her a quick, hard kiss. "The sooner we get to the safety of Kotoyeesinay, the sooner we can pick this up where we left off. If that's what you want."

"Hell, yes. I want to lick you like a lollipop." She'd only had three lovers in her life and had never been bold when it came to sex, but Trevor was changing her outlook. "I need you inside me like I need water."

His eyes darkened with desire and he groaned. "You're killing me."

"Back at you." She made herself take three steps back, so she couldn't touch him. "I'll pack everything and raid the vending machine while you make arrangements for your trailer."

"Deal." He gave her an assessing look. "How's your knee?"

"Getting better by the minute." She pointed to her belly. "Junior here helps me heal quickly, though not as fast a full shifter."

He smiled. "Junior is a girl, in case you didn't know. I can smell her."

"She is?" Her eyes widened, and anger sparked. "Those lying feline sons of bitches swore they didn't know the baby's sex." She shook her head. "Get on with you, then. I'll be ready when you are."

Jackie had to admit that riding in a wide, well-padded bucket seat, high above the traffic, was miles better than riding a motorcycle. After Trevor had disconnected his trailer, which he'd assured her had only furniture, he'd used rope and a couple of tie-downs to strap her scraped and bent, but hopefully repairable, motorcycle to the back of his truck.

They made excellent time on the highway, especially since it was a weekend. She'd lost all track of days and calendars. She was in comfortable clothes for summertime, and could stretch anytime she wanted, or change position when Junior... or Princess, she guessed, kicked.

Periodically, she checked the threat map, which she'd adjusted so it showed all the time. At their present rate, and assuming Trevor's luck was better than hers—whose wasn't? —they'd be into the canyon that led to Kotoyeesinay by the time Roehm's hunters crossed the state border. Of concern was the fact that the red swarm had veered to the west, toward the mountains, instead of going due north as they had been.

She didn't know how to use her magic to tell her why the change. Talismans worked best if the object being enchanted had a similar mundane purpose, such as finding the best route. She'd fallen out of practice using her magic while concealing it from the non-magical humans in Houston, and then she'd been afraid to use it in Roehm's compound, in case he'd purchased warning or detection spells. He had no free magic, but he knew how to buy it from others. It had taken her a month of stolen moments to charge the rusty pipe she'd made into her weapon.

"Do we have time to stop in Laramie for fuel?" He tapped one of the many gauges on the wrap-around console arrayed in front of him. "We can make it with what we've got, but I'd like to have a cushion."

She considered the map. "Yeah, if we're fast. We're still a couple of hours ahead of them." She rolled her eyes. "I need a bathroom, again, and some chocolate milk. What can I get for you?"

"Noth..." He trailed off. He glanced at her, a slow smile lighting up his face. "Condoms."

She gave an exaggerated gasp of surprise. "A fine, sexy man like you doesn't have condoms in every pocket? The women in your life must have been blind." She laughed to cover the small spike of jealousy that lanced through her. "I'll buy a box of extra-large, just to be safe."

"Buy two boxes." His tone had a touch of growly bear in it that zinged straight to her core. "Just hearing you breathe gives me wood."

She loved the idea that she turned him on, but she knew it wasn't just her charming self. "I'm sorry about the shifter-mate pheromones thing. I've been thinking about a spell to mask it. I don't want to be a magnet for every horny shifter within smelling distance the rest of my life."

Princess chose that moment to kick twice in her belly. "Damn, child, give me a break."

After their brief visit to the Laramie truck stop, she opened the new Wyoming map she'd bought and tried a new spell she'd been thinking about. This time, she spoke their desired destination, then waved her hand over the map. The fastest route showed up as a yellow line, and the safest route showed up as a blue line. The lines disagreed on which exit to take, but they converged at the foothills, where the road began curving into the switchback canyon. The only alternate route, shown in green, would take them on a long and circuitous path north, west, and then east.

She showed the map to Trevor, who had her put it next to the threat map on the clipboard he'd rigged for easy reference. She made the traffic map into a talisman that displayed continuously.

He grinned at her. "After we get out of all this mess, I'm hiring you to do that for all my maps."

It was nice having her small magical talent valued instead of disbelieved or laughed at. "Gladly, but your money's no good with me, mister. I owe you more than I could possibly repay."

His smile faded. "You don't owe me for doing the right thing."

She didn't know how to respond. She downed the last of the chocolate milk and flattened the small carton for the trash.

In her experience, damn few people did the right thing just because. The people in the rural hometown she'd fled wouldn't know the right thing if it smacked them upside the head. A statistics professor at her junior college traded grades for cash and made a mint because most students flunked the class the first time. Her fellow university students assumed she'd gotten her scholarship because of the color of her skin, not her flawless academic record. As a certified public accountant, she'd lost count of the number of clients who squirmed when she wouldn't sign off on dubious tax shelters or unethical financial deals.

Still, her mother held her head high and helped people in need, even when they'd been viciously hateful to her. Her boss respected her opinion and backed her every time a client wanted to switch to a more "flexible" accountant. And compassionate, sinfully sexy Trevor helped her, instead of turning away or taking advantage. Every additional minute she spent with him had her reevaluating her plans for her future, because she wanted it to include him.

She looked away from his handsome profile to focus on the rocky slopes outside the passenger window. She hadn't told him everything, and he might not want anything to do with her once she did. The last six months had destroyed her belief that she'd always do the right thing, no matter what.

He cleared his throat. "What do you know about true mates for shifters?"

She glanced at him, but he was focused on taking the sloping exit for the fastest route to get to the winding road to Kotoyeesinay.

Unease curled in her gut. "Roehm told his pride there's no such thing, and the only thing females are good for is sex-mating for cubs, but he lies about everything. The pride's cheetah shifter cuts himself every night until he passes out from blood loss, crying for his dead mate." She slid one hand over her rounded stomach. "Barry said he was my mate."

She tightened a fist to keep the tears at bay. She'd already cried too much for the life she could never go back to. "I thought he'd been kidnapped for the auction, too, but then I overheard the staff saying they had to sell me quick. Seems the leopard who'd delivered me forgot to mention I was pregnant, which they figured was why he'd taken such a low price." She unclenched her aching hand and flattened her fingers on her thigh. "So, if that's what a mate is, I'll pass."

"That's not what a mate is." He shook his head and drummed fingers on the steering wheel. "No more than a sleazy, cheating slimeball human with two families and a mistress on the side is a husband."

"Hah! You must have met the former mayor of Weirtree." She made a hissing sound. "The only reason he's not still the mayor is his pregnant mistress shot him in the ass when she realized he wasn't leaving his wife. Then she told the state's attorney general about the dock on the gulf where he kept his boat and his slush fund." She shook her head. "Before all this, I was saving every penny, so I could move my mother to live in Houston, away from all that holierthan-thou, good-old-boy crap." Her eyes ached from unshed tears. "I can't ever go back. Who knows what Barry told them. Everyone probably thinks I'm dead."

"That totally sucks." The truck slowed to a stop at the intersection, and he glanced at her. "I won't pretend shifters are angels. We're driven by dual instincts, man and beast. Prides, packs, and clans have to maintain secrecy to protect us from human fear and enforce the discipline that human society can't. We have our share of greed and evil, just like any other magical species, though I can't say we flattened a forest in Siberia like the arctic elf and winter fairy war did."

He turned left toward the higher mountains and picked up speed. "But mates..." He waved his fingers and took a deep breath. "True mates—some call them fated mates—are part physical, part mental, part destiny. They're our survival. Mated shifters gain better control of their nature and power, meaning they're more likely to settle down, less likely to get themselves killed doing reckless things. It's more than just smokin' hot sex, though that's a part of it. Shifter mate magic is life-changing." His jaw tightened. "A true-mated shifter wouldn't abandon his pregnant mate unless he was dead. And maybe not even then."

The deep conviction in his voice struck a resonant chord. It was still possible that Barry was innocent, that some other leopard shifter had sold her to the auction house, but in her heart, she knew he'd done it. When she'd finally realized no one was coming to rescue her, and the poorly insulated mobile home had been so cold she couldn't sleep, she'd come to realize Barry had treated her like a favorite sex doll to play with when he was in the mood, or shove in the closet when he wasn't.

"Barry wasn't my mate." It felt so good to say it that she repeated it. "Barry Wills was a selfish, conniving bastard who couldn't even remember my birthday, and he wasn't my mate."

Trevor nodded. "And I'll lay odds that Roehm is as damaged as his pride. He probably can't even feel the mate bond in others, so he thinks it's a myth. He'd have gotten rid of any mated pairs first because their bond made them stronger, and their very existence proved he's defective."

"He's way beyond defective." She turned away from the memories of how he'd treated his people. "He's violent and dangerous, and he'll want me back. Don't underestimate him."

"I won't." Trevor's expression morphed into grim distaste. "I thought you were 'owned' by Ricardo and Ruben."

"I was." She really didn't want to have this conversation, but she couldn't continue to keep Trevor in the dark. He deserved to know, and to make his own choices.

"I worked my way into cleaning for everyone except Roehm, who didn't trust anyone in his space. I mimicked the submissive behavior of the other captives, so the pride would think I was harmless." She caught herself rounding her shoulders even as she mentioned it. She only noticed it now because she hadn't felt the need since Trevor had come to get her after the accident.

"About two months ago, Roehm needed to impress another shifter leader he wanted to do business with. He realized his office and personal area now looked like shit compared to the rest of the compound. He ordered me to do for him and watched me like a hawk the whole time. He'd just torn apart one of the lynx-shifter boys that morning, so I didn't have to pretend to be terrified of him." She took a deep breath and blew out the flash of fear. She was in a nice, cozy truck with a big, protective bear. Man. Whatever.

"After that, he had me come in every other day. A couple of weeks goes by, and I'm still meek and scared. He's bored watching and starts leaving me alone for longer and longer. I started snooping whenever I could. That's when I found his ledger."

"Ledger?" asked Trevor. "That sounds more organized than I was giving him credit for."

"Yeah, me, too. He makes a big show of keeping important papers and floppy disks in a walk-in safe in his office. It and his personal computer have mundane and magical alarms, and he mentions them often. That's the distraction." She made a flourish with her fingers like a stage magician. "I found the ledgers in the middle of some old paper files from the former leader's days. Roehm has been robbing the pride blind, while keeping them at barely above poverty level, with occasional big parties when the grumbling gets too loud."

"What did you do?"

"Nothing, then." Now came the less pleasant part. "I was stealing from the pride, too. Everyone I cleaned for, even if they were as poor as me. Money, clothes, maps, anything I thought would be useful for an escape. I had stashes all over. When I saw it was too dangerous to steal any of the pride's community vehicles, I convinced Ricardo and Ruben to buy themselves a motorcycle, so they wouldn't have to ask Roehm for permission just to go get booze. Then I made those lazy asses think it was their idea to teach me how to drive it, so I could go get the booze for them."

"That was incredibly smart." He shook his head. "You're a stronger alpha than I am. I'd have probably tried muscling my way out of the compound and gotten myself killed for it. I don't like fighting."

That startled her. "I'm no alpha, I'm a coward." She made herself add the worst part. "And a murderer."

His gasp didn't surprise her. He was a deeply honorable man. She'd once been an honorable woman, too.

"Bullshit," he growled.

She looked at him in shock.

He spared her a quick glance. "Who did you kill—Roehm?"

"No." She fidgeted with the placket of her shirt. "Roehm promised the pride an all-night bash. He also invited a New Mexico wolf pack he wanted an alliance with to come party with them, meaning he'd have to deactivate the magic perimeter wards. Couldn't have some drunk wolf stumble into them and get fried. I saw it as my last opportunity for escape because I was getting too fat to run." She twisted her fingers together over her belly. "Everything went according to plan until Ruben caught me dressed for the escape, loading the motorcycle's saddlebags with everything I'd stolen. He hit and kicked me, but he was so drunk, he could barely stand. I pleaded with him to just let me leave, but all he could talk about was the reward from Roehm. He fell on his hands and knees. Before he could get up, I pulled the bowie knife out of his belt sheath and slit his throat from ear to ear." She took a deep breath to let out the tension. "I left him on the ground, bleeding out, and rode out like a bat out of hell. The only thing Roehm was ever afraid of was the Shifter Tribunal in Chicago, so that's where I plan to go. They might take my illegal shifter child away, but at least they'll look into Roehm's activities."

Trevor growled deep in his throat. "There's no such thing as an illegal shifter child."

"Right, just like there's no auction for humans with shifter-mate potential." She shook her head. "I know most of the stories I heard from Roehm and his degenerates are a load of crap, but there's no way a shifter judge would let an ordinary human keep and raise a leopard-shifter child." She couldn't stop the tears. "I've tried so hard not to get attached, because either she was going to auction or some proper shifter family, but I love her." She dropped her head back on the seat and let the tears flow. "I love her so much."

"Fuck, fuck, fuck!" Trevor's voice penetrated the downward spiral of her misery. "Where's a fucking turnoff when you need one?"

His male impatience made her smile a little. She pointed to his clipboard. "Ask the magic map."

She took a deep, watery breath and let it out with an audible sigh. Trevor's hand appeared before her, holding a wad of tissues. She took them and used one to blow her nose. She half smiled when it sounded like an out-of-tune trumpet. One of her mother's perennial jokes.

The truck slowed. She looked up to see a sign for a wildlife viewing area ahead. She wondered if mountain-dwelling shifters pranced around for the tourists, just to give them something to talk about.

Luck was with them, because the dirt road was easily wide enough for his truck, and bonus, it had a lone portable toilet standing at one end of the split-rail fence.

She sealed up her jacket against the ever-present wind, then opened the passenger door. Before she could move, he was standing on the running board and scooping her into his arms, then stepping down to place her on the ground. "I know you need to go, but we're talking when you get back." The wonderful man handed her a roll of toilet paper.

Jackie snuggled into Trevor's lap, feeling guilty for enjoying it so much. "We can talk while you drive, you know." They sat on the long, narrow bed in the cab's sleeping compartment that she hadn't known was behind her.

He tightened his arms around her, and sound rumbled from his chest. "Not for this, we can't." He kissed her temple. "First things first. You're not a murderer, any more than a captured soldier is a murderer because he kills the enemy. End of fucking story."

"Uhm, okay. But I still killed a man." She couldn't bring herself to feel bad that Ruben had died, but she'd remember the wet, gurgling sound for the rest of her life.

"It was you or him. I'm glad you won." He kissed her head again. "Second, you are definitely an alpha. The best alphas know when to use their minds instead of muscles. There's always someone who can beat you in a fight, or can outthink you, but damn few who know the right time to use each or both. That's you. Anyone can die. It takes tremendous heart and courage to live."

"I was scared all the time." She breathed in the soothing scent of him. "They smelled it on me."

"You should have been scared. The difference was, you didn't let it stop you. If I'm ever caught behind enemy lines, I want you with me, because I know you'll get us out."

"I appreciate your confidence." She touched the side of his jaw, where his beard would grow if he let it. "If it's all right with you, I'd like to avoid any wars."

"Me, too. I like peace." He moved to kiss her a third time, but she twisted so he kissed her lips instead of her temple. He tasted so very good, and the bed beneath them gave her ideas on how best to use the small space, but she wanted to hear what he had to say. She pulled back to catch her breath.

He cradled her face in his palm and caught her gaze. "Third, whatever else happens, I will fight with every resource I have so you can keep your baby."

She was honored by the stubborn determination behind his pledge. "Thank you." She knew life was never that simple, but it warmed the depths of her soul to know he'd be in her corner. She caught a whiff of smoke. "Is something burning?"

He looked past her, and his eyes widened. "The threat map!"

She pushed off his lap so he could lunge for the cab. With lightning speed, he grabbed a bottled water and doused the scorching paper.

She moved closer, so she could see what went wrong with her magic. Unfortunately, it was just physics. A new swarm of red, coming from Laramie, had converged with the Colorado swarm into a hot, moving mass that was only an hour behind them at best.

She scrambled into her seat and fastened her seatbelt. "How fast can this thing go?"

He started the engine and fastened his, as well. "We're about to find out."

4
___

Trevor muttered a litany of curses as he decelerated for yet another sharp curve that he couldn't see around. It meant going slowly enough to stay in his lane, so as not to scare the life out of any oncoming traffic and cause an accident.

"The threat map says those three red 'scout' dots are really close. We should be able to see them soon." She'd been alternating between watching the map and turning to look behind them.

Jackie sounded tense, but not panicked, which helped keep his bear from worrying about her. His mate was one hell of a magnificent woman. He wasn't anywhere good enough for her, but he aimed to become so. If she'd have him. If they lived long enough.

With its big engine and no load, his truck had made great time, until the road narrowed and started winding. He didn't remember the mountainsides being so steep and rocky the last time he'd been through there.

"Could I try an experimental spell on your passenger-side mirror? If it works, it'll show us the first vehicles behind us, regardless of how far back they are."

"Go for it." The sun had been high in the sky, but now, it was tilting west and creating shaded sections on the road. The sharp contrasts dazzled his human eyes, so he borrowed a bit of his bear to compensate. Being an alpha, with the half-shift capabilities it brought, had its advantages, even if he had no clan to serve and lead.

A brief pulse against his magical senses came from Jackie as she rolled down the window and touched the big mirror.

"What the hell?" Her consternation was plain.

He slowed for another blind curve and ignored the temptation to take his eyes from the road. "What?"

"It's three men on low-slung motorcycles, like right out of the old movie Easy Rider."

A bus-sized recreational vehicle rounded the bend in front of him at a dangerously fast speed and veered into his lane. He cursed and steered his truck as far right as he dared. At the last possible second, the RV recovered and swerved back into its own lane. He was tempted to blast his loud air horn, but the jerk was already gone.

"The motorcycles just passed the 'falling rocks' sign. They'll see us soon on one of the mountain curves." She made a frustrated sound. "The map shows they're a threat, but Roehm hasn't done business with anyone in Wyoming."

He took advantage of a comparatively long and straight stretch to accelerate. "Maybe they're meaning to attack Kotoyeesinay, and we're just in their way."

"Maybe"—she pointed to the map—"but the town still shows bright blue. It should show red if it's trouble for us."

Up ahead, the mountains rose steeper. A curve revealed part of the road on the next hill, and two more cars coming down, including a vintage Jaguar that was zipping around the slower modern Cadillac. Fates deliver him from cretins in convertibles who thought narrow mountain roads were their own Grand Prix course. "Where is all this traffic coming from?"

"It's the end of a summer weekend," Jackie said. "And besides, didn't you say the town has a casino? Rich people like to gamble. Barry sure did."

The threat map showed the red swarm creeping closer. "Do you have a spell that can make us invisible?"

"No, sorry. I can't hide something as big as your truck."

He took the inside curve more slowly than he wanted because he didn't trust the oncoming traffic would see him in time. Fortunately, the two cars went by without any trouble. He almost missed the small sign that said five miles to Kotoyeesinay. Encouraging, but a hell of a lot of road for trouble to catch up to them.

"Besides," she continued, "if we were invisible, we'd be a worse traffic hazard than those Hell's Angels wannabes behind us." She leaned closer to her window to stare at the mirror. "Oh, shit. I recognize those vests. That's what Wiley the coyote and his fur-butt drinking buddy wore."

He cursed. "How did they find us?"

"Good question. Are the coyotes working with Roehm and his Mad Max rejects, or do they want something else? And how did Roehm find us?"

"Mad Max?" He downshifted and hugged the lane divider on the outside curve. His bear might be fine going down the side of a mountain, but his truck wouldn't fare so well. Neither would his mate.

She made a rude sound. "Muscle cars with spike grills, Jeeps with harpoons on top-mount turrets, you name it. The pride has a chop shop in the compound where they break down stolen cars for parts. Their hobby is customizing the pride's vehicles."

"Great." He slowed for a hairpin turn that would take them higher up the mountain. "The fates hate me."

"It's not as bad as it sounds. Roehm drove off the only talented mechanic they had. The rest of them barely know which end of a welder to point away from their face."

"They can still cause us a world of hurt." He glanced quickly at her before focusing on the road. "Does Roehm want you dead or alive?"

"Alive, because..." She swore a loud, vicious oath. "I'm a bonehead. I know how he found us. He's using a purchased tracking spell to follow the ledger. I was going to turn them over to the Shifter Tribunal as evidence. I used my magic to hide them from sight in my saddle bags, but not from magical sight."

She twisted and fished behind her seat as he navigated a hairpin turn. He felt her magic flare like a sensuous brush of velvet on his skin. "They're truly hidden now, but it doesn't help us much. They already know where we are."

"Yeah, and they've probably guessed we're going to Kotoyeesinay." He punched the accelerator. "Our best hope is to get there first."

Out of the corner of his eye, he saw her lean forward toward the side mirror again. "The motorcycles just passed that big RV. One of them turned back to follow it."

"Maybe they don't know what vehicle they're looking for, so they have to check the drivers." He took the next turn faster than he should have, but he felt the pressure of their pursuit.

"Could also be a coincidence. We still don't know how they're tracking us." She blew out a loud breath. "I wish I was better at magic. Princess lends me her strength, but that doesn't help me think of better ways to use it."

"Princess?" He understood even as he said it. "Your daughter."

"Didn't think she'd appreciate being called Junior any longer." Her voice held a note of sadness in the humor.

He wished he could spare a hand to touch her, comfort her. Soon, he promised his whining bear. "We'll ask her when she's old enough," he said firmly.

She was silent a long moment. "You really are a wonderful man." Her voice had the watery quality that meant her tears were flowing again.

He forced himself to pay attention to his driving. "Can your magic mirror see how many motorcycles we're dealing with? We know there are more than just the three men you saw before, right?"

"Yes, they'd have a lot more riders, to make that clump on the threat map. And no, I can't see them. The mirror is a fixed view." She sniffled as she grabbed the pen off his clipboard and tore a page off his notepad. "But I have an idea."

He concentrated on the road. He'd thought they were headed toward a summit, but it turned out to be the foothill to a much larger mountain. Its familiar look cheered him, because he'd been worried they'd somehow taken a wrong turn and were going the long way around.

The sustained flare of her magic caressed him like she'd stuck her hand down his pants. No one else's magic had that effect on him. Apparently being around his mate returned him to the days of being a constantly horny shifter teenager.

"Okay, if this worked right, we have thirteen motorcycles after us. Two are really close, and one is heading back to the rest. The big clump is riding two-up."

A clear view of a long stretch of empty curved road had him accelerating and crossing into the opposite lane to hug the mountainside. A small sign said two miles to Kotoyeesinay.

"There they are." Jackie was turned, looking out the side window. "That's what, a mile back?"

"About." He couldn't go any faster or they'd miss the turnoff. He couldn't remember if it was left or right.

"One of them pointed toward us. They're speeding up."

Another curve meant he had to get back in his lane. He took a deep breath to release tension, but it didn't help. The red on the threat map glowed like a raging wildfire.

"Coyote One and Two are gaining." After a moment, she added, "Shit, the mirror just showed me Roehm's spike-grill Charger."

He suppressed a growl. "Do they have any long-range weapons? Guns? Grenade launchers?"

"They mostly sold handguns and rifles. I don't know what a grenade launcher looks like. The coyotes aren't wearing holsters or anything."

Finally, he saw the turnoff sign he'd been looking for. "Left turn coming up fast. Hang on to anything that might go flying."

He couldn't spare her a glance because it took all his concentration not to tilt sideways as he slowed to take the turn. Big-engine tractor trucks depended on rear weight to keep them from being unstable land rockets on ten tires.

The road turned out to be wider than he'd imagined, and well paved. It also appeared to be headed around the mountain and down. He couldn't remember how far it was to town. He sped up as much as he dared and watched for road hazards and traffic.

"Coyote One missed the turn, but Coyote Two didn't.

He's on our tail." She leaned toward the side mirror. "I think he's got a CB radio, because he's talking into a microphone."

Trevor tilted his chin toward his unit on the console. "Use that and see if you can find what band he's using. Try nineteen first."

After some fumbling, she found the volume and channel dials. They both jumped at the sudden burst of static, then a man's loud voice.

"...almost caught up. He's got a female with him."

"Right behind you," came another man's voice. "Get in front..."

A third, female voice interrupted. "Don't be stupid. Pull off where you are. We'll catch up."

"But if he gets to Kotoyeesinay, we can't touch him." That was the loud man.

"We'll petition the town council. He's gotta pay," the woman growled. "Don't cross the border or hurt him on glade lands, or they'll hurt us worse."

The truck crested a hill, then began a steep descent. Trevor downshifted to keep the truck under control.

"Is it, uh, against the shifter code to tell me what's going on?"

"No, but I have no idea why they're chasing me." Trees rose up around them as the road curved into what looked like a forested valley. It looked inviting and forbidding at the same time. "I didn't do anything else to the two that jumped you like I wanted to."

The woman's voice came back on. "Watch out for that Jeep with the turret. Morgan got a whiff of lynx when they passed us. None of 'em can drive for shit."

"The Charger just blew past us. About five more just made the turnoff."

"If they're after our bear," growled the woman, "they'll have to stand in line."

A powerful wave of magic flowed over the truck and through Trevor. Reality wavered, and suddenly, he felt like he'd walked into a tuxedo affair buck naked, with everyone giving him the once over. The real world snapped back in time for him to hear Jackie gasp and curse. He'd forgotten to warn her about the border effect. He'd also forgotten to tell her his aunt's instructions.

"Jackie, we have to ask for sanctuary." He downshifted again, then spoke loud and clear. "I am Trevor Hammond, and I ask the Kotoyeesinay glade for sanctuary."

She cleared her throat. "I am Jacqueline Breton, and I ask the Kotoyeesinay glade for sanctuary for me and my unborn daughter. And for Trevor."

He couldn't tell if their words had an effect. The road narrowed around a hairpin turn that took them around a thirty-foot-high boulder.

"Uhm, I think that rock just waved at you." She sounded dubious.

"Could be. A couple of the rock giants take shifts as sentinels." Another hairpin turn, this time in the opposite direction. He remembered this part of the road because it seemed to defy real-world geometry. He'd found it best not to think about it, and just go with the flow.

They passed through a time-weathered formation that looked like a rough-hewn gouge in the mountainside. Suddenly, they were in a valley that spread down and out before them like a sculpted ocean of boulders surrounded by green and purple wildflowers. The town of Kotoyeesinay nestled in among tall trees in the far end, looking cozy and sleepy in the afternoon sun.

"That's amazing," breathed Jackie.

Trevor eased up on the accelerator. "We should be safe—"

The truck jerked like a bucking bronco. He tightened his grip on the twisting steering wheel and fought to stay on the road. Another jerk, this time with the sound of tearing metal.

Jackie peered into her big side mirror. "Fucking hell! It's Roehm's Jeep. They just harpooned my motorcycle and pulled it off the back of your truck."

Trevor punched the accelerator. The engine roared in response, and the scenery almost blurred. In front of them, the road seemed to widen and lengthen, as if to give him room for a race.

"Those morons just ran over..." She rolled down the window and twisted in her seat to look back, then turned to look at him. "Er, I think a dragon just scooped up the Jeep like an eagle taking a rabbit." She shook her head. "If I'm not hallucinating."

"You aren't." He let the truck slow as he pointed up ahead, where the motorcycle dangled from the Jeep clutched in the bronze-colored dragon's talons. "The glade takes security very seriously."

He slowed to an even more sedate pace as several more metallic-hued dragons rose and flew over them. He expected the others from Roehm's gang were about to get a similar welcome.

"I hope dragons are bulletproof. Roehm likes to shoot things."

The road curved and inclined gently to the northwest, toward the town. "He's a real piece of work, isn't he?" Trevor stole several quick glances at Jackie's profile as she stared straight ahead, toward the decorated wrought-iron arch over the road that spelled out the name of the town in ornate letters. She looked scared and worried. "You're not alone. I'll be with you the whole time." He poured every ounce of resolve he possessed into his words. No matter what happened, his place was by her side.

She glanced at him, startled, then shook her head. "It's still weird that you know what I'm thinking." She smiled briefly. "But I like it."

Once past the welcoming arch, he slowed to the speed limit as Glade Road became the town's main thoroughfare. "No point in going to Shepherd's garage now, I guess. How about we head straight for Town Hall?" He pointed toward the three-story building that rose above the town's roofline.

"Yes. Let's get this over with." She blew out a noisy breath. "I don't want anyone else hurt because of me."

Trevor ached to hold her, to tell her what she meant to him, but he didn't think she'd believe him. They might be temporarily safe from their immediate pursuers, but they weren't even close to being out of the woods. And in a golden elf glade, the woods could be deadly.

Well, so could he. He'd promised her not to do something stupid and get himself killed, but he damn sure intended to protect her with everything he had, because she was everything to him.

5

J ackie felt like she was back in college, when she'd had to present her undergraduate capstone term paper to a pair of bored professors. This time, however, she was in the asphalt parking lot outside the Kotoyeesinay town hall, speaking before a hastily assembled town council of six, seated behind a folding conference table. A magic-infused, twenty-foot-long ground tarp served as a witness box. Anyone standing on it could be heard far and wide, even when whispering. She and Trevor stood together in a defensive magic circle of chalk near the tarp's north edge.

Jackie probably would have fainted dead away by now if it hadn't been for Trevor. The moment they'd left his truck, he'd swallowed her in a long, tension-draining bear hug. After her quick visit to the town hall's bathrooms and drinking fountains, he'd kept her close as they explained the events that brought them to ask for sanctuary.

She'd be lying if she said she hadn't enjoyed being near him, or him initiating contact as often as he did. He was the only anchor she had in a reality gone seriously askew.

Kotoyeesinay looked like any of the mountain towns she'd passed through during her escape, with ordinary streets and a normal mix of architecture. Its denizens were anything but.

The six council members sat at the eight-foot table. Behind them stood a small red-and-silver, two-legged dragon with bat-like wings, and a dark-skinned centaur male who made Clydesdales look like ponies. It was hard not to stare. They were all right out of the fantasy stories she'd devoured as a child, and better than anything movie special-effects artists could dream up. She didn't even recognize half of the species in the gathering onlookers.

The meeting was outside because neither the motorcycle-mounted coyotes nor Roehm's pissed-off pride were willing to leave their vehicles unguarded around the other group. The coyotes, especially the females, laughed at the pride's post-apocalyptic vehicles and insulted the virility of the felines, who snarled vile insults back. A pair of Roehm's lynx enforcers flatly refused to leave their vehicle altogether, once they saw the red dragon. Jackie couldn't blame them since the roof of their jeep still had a gaping tear from where a dragon had clawed off the harpoon gun.

A slim, dazzlingly beautiful golden elf female stood in the center behind the council table. Her clothing seemed to be made of living red-leaf ferns and mosses. An intricate tiara of carved wood held her brass-green hair away from her delicate features. Her eyes said she was far, far older than the teenager she resembled. She watched with apparent disinterest as Roehm and one of the coyote women strode up to the ground tarp from their respective sides.

Two translucent creatures in ghostly armor lowered very real and sharp scimitars to prevent Roehm and the woman from stepping onto the tarp.

The golden elf gestured toward the woman. "We will hear Alpha Zarabitta's petition first." More elven magic carried her soft voice right to Jackie's ear, as if she stood within a few feet. That didn't startle Jackie nearly as much as the fact that the coyotes' leader was a confident, muscled, and curvy female. Both Jackie's ex-lover Barry and Roehm had insisted no male shifter would ever accept a female as alpha. Of course, they'd proven time and again to be liars.

Zarabitta blew Roehm a smart-ass kiss as she stepped forward. Roehm's lip twisted sourly, but he dropped back a few paces. He could pretend to follow the rules of others when it suited him.

Jackie's back spasmed with tension. She wished she could sit, but then she'd never see anything. Trevor stepped behind her and pulled her gently against him, wordlessly urging her to relax. His arms wrapped around her, and she allowed herself the comfort of his presence. She didn't know how it was possible, but she was falling for a man she'd only met the day before. That he was also a shifter didn't seem to matter anymore. He was a good bear and an honorable, sexy man.

Zarabitta gave a respectful short bow toward the council. "I give thanks to Guivre Gul-Vert and the council for our guest pass into the glade." Her powerful alto voice had depth and a hint of smoky-bar rasp. "I'll get straight to the point. Yesterday, with no provocation whatsoever, that bear"—Zarabitta pointed accusingly at her and Trevor —"jumped two of my pack behind Otto's in Cheyenne and left them for dead. We spotted him this morning in Laramie and followed him here."

Jackie took an outraged breath to object but stopped when Trevor tightened his arms around her. "Wait," he whispered. His warm breath in her ear sent a delicious thrill through her. Honestly, her body picked the worst times to take up its own agenda.

"And what do you want with him now?" asked the golden elf.

Zarabitta put her hands on her hips. "Blood for blood. Our training barn."

Jackie didn't like the sound of that. She remembered schoolyard fights, and how bullies had preyed on the weaker kids. Trevor's bear was impressive, but even he couldn't take on a whole pack.

A handsome lavender-skinned male fairy with sharp features and flashing amethyst eyes stepped out from behind the table. His clothes of draped velvet and lace made him seem frivolous, but the thin wand in his hand belied that. Even from twenty feet away, Jackie could feel the magical power emanating from it. "Consent for a geas spell of truth-speaking?"

Zarabitta frowned. "Yeah, as long as you don't go fishing for stuff that's none of your business. But I wasn't at Otto's."

The male with the wand paused and looked toward Guivre, who tilted her head slightly. "Are the injured parties with you now, that we may hear their tale?"

Zarabitta nodded, then turned toward the motorcycles and whistled loudly enough to make Jackie wince. "Wiley! Cody! Get your asses front and center."

Jackie rarely wished she was taller, but this was one of those times. She couldn't see anything over the heads of the swelling crowd that had stopped to watch the proceedings. Sounds of a commotion arose from near the motorcycles. Jackie twisted in Trevor's arms to give him a questioning look. He shrugged and shook his head.

Finally, after long minutes, the crowd parted, and three vest-wearing coyote shifters half-dragged, half-carried Wiley and the other shifter who'd come onto her at the truck stop into view. They shoved them onto the tarp.

Zarabitta stomped toward them. Jackie couldn't see her face, but her stiff shoulders and fisted hands didn't bode well for Wiley or Cody.

"This is your third strike, assholes," Zarabitta bit out. "If you don't tell me right fucking now why you were running and what really happened yesterday, I will feed you to the wyvern myself." She pointed a thumb toward the red-and-silver reptile behind the council table. The red dragon... wyvern tested the air with a snake-like forked tongue, then snorted wetly.

Wiley hung his head and said nothing. Cody crossed his arms and jutted out his chin. "It's too late. Dad's already reported you to the Shifter Tribunal." He sneered and spat within inches of Zarabitta's dusty boots. "Bitches belong in the den with the pups. You ain't even mated."

Zarabitta shook her head. "Your dad has ruined you." She nodded, and two of the coyote shifters latched onto Cody's arms. "You're out, Cody. You and your father are exiled for good." A wave of unknown shifter magic passed by Jackie. Cody shuddered hard from head to toe, and the color drained from his face. He whined a curse.

The two grim-faced coyotes dragged Cody away, ignoring his angry protests and threats.

Zarabitta turned to Wiley. "You have a hard choice to make, son, and not much time." She tilted her chin toward the direction Cody had gone. "He's your only litter mate, but he and your dad are mean drunks. You go with them, you'll either be their meal ticket, or you'll become them." She pointed a thumb toward the Kotoyeesinay council. "Tell us all the truth, and you can stay. You'll be on shit patrol for a while, 'cause you fucked up big time, but you've got a good heart."

Zarabitta backed up two steps and stood, arms crossed. The only sound was the afternoon breeze through the aspen trees and the pounding of Jackie's heart.

Wiley looked up at Zarabitta, then shot a glance at Jackie before casting his eyes down again. He shoved his hands in his pockets. "Cody was drunk. We wanted to party with that woman, 'cause we thought she was a prostitute. She ran like prey. We chased. Her bear mate knocked us around and commanded us to shift back to human, then left with her. Dad found us in the alley and beat the shit out of us for being pansies." Wiley seemed to shrink in on himself. "When we caught scent of the bear again, Dad got the idea to send us all off on the chase, while he told the Tribunal you and the pack went rogue. He's gonna declare himself alpha, with Cody as his second." His glance flickered toward where Cody could still be heard shouting. "Cody said we had to run, or the elves would make us into pets like that red dragon."

The wyvern raised its long, sinuous neck and extended its wings. "I am a wyvern, you cretin." Its refined, upper-crust British accent held deep outrage. "I am no one's pet."

Jackie rubbed her arms where the sibilant hiss under the words raised atavistic goosebumps across her skin.

Zarabitta turned and bowed toward the wyvern. "My apologies, Scholar of the Skies. Wiley has shit for brains, but he meant no offense."

The wyvern's wings folded, and then it relaxed with a disgruntled "harrumph." Jackie bit her lip to keep from laughing.

Zarabitta crossed to the center of the tarp and nodded to Jackie and Trevor, then turned and bowed to the council. "I withdraw my request for custody of the bear shifter named Trevor Hammond. We further acknowledge a debt of succor and defense to both him and his future mate, that they may pass on to their immediate offspring."

A murmur arose from the crowd, and all eyes turned toward her and Trevor. She didn't have a clue what to say, but thankfully, Trevor did. "No harm done. The debt is acknowledged, and the proposed recompense is accepted." He tightened his arms around her and whispered in her ear. "I'll explain later."

Zarabitta nodded, then turned again to the council. "With your permission, we'd like to ride out." From near the motorcycles, Cody's howl changed from human to pure coyote. Zarabitta's eyes rolled. "Seems I have den cleaning to do."

The beautiful golden elf nodded. "Farewell, Alpha Leader. Follow the right will-o-the-wisp, and your road will be straight and true."

Zarabitta bowed again, then strode purposefully toward Wiley and the other coyote, who fell in behind her as she passed. They were swallowed by the crowd as Zarabitta shouted, "Someone tie that moron's muzzle shut!"

From the far side of the tarp, Roehm and five of his pride watched the action. They looked like extras in a low-budget post-apocalyptic movie. Roehm fixed Jackie with a confident, malevolent stare that promised a slow and painful death. Her first instinct was to hunch into a submissive posture and look away, but Trevor's strong arms and his deep, throaty rumbling behind her gave her the courage to stand up straight and look Roehm right in the eye. A frown crossed his face, before he smoothed his expression. He put one toe on the tarp and looked at the golden elf female. "Is it my turn?" His tone bordered on insolent.

At Guivre's nod, the ghostly guard's scimitar in front of Roehm rose. He headed straight for the middle of the tarp, as if taking center stage. His metal-studded leather jacket tightened as his arms and chest bulged. At well over six feet and heavily muscled, he radiated prime alpha dominance and barely contained berserker rage. The power beat against her temple, like it wanted into her brain. She put her hands protectively over her belly.

Guivre yawned.

The council members tittered and covered their mouths to hide their smiles. The lavender fairy smirked. The centaur outright laughed. Jackie only just stopped her jaw from dropping.

Roehm's veneer of civility cracked. He pointed an accusing finger at Jackie. "That human skank stole stuff from me and my pride. She slit the throat of her owner... uh, landlord and stole his motorcycle. She has to pay. Hand her over, and no one gets hurt."

Guivre tilted her head, almost bird-like. "Have you an invitation?"

Roehm sneered. "I don't need an invitation. I have a crew." He pointed a thumb toward his pride members, all enforcers, but kept his eyes trained on the golden elf. "Give 'em a taste, boys. Shift!"

Jackie felt Roehm's shifter magic command and instinctively covered her stomach with her arms. In the past, the command to shift had given her a powerful cramp, as if her baby was trying to obey, but this time, the magic slid on by her like an errant breeze. Behind her, the deep growl vibrating Trevor's chest soothed her.

The enforcers stayed human. They looked at one

another, surprised, as if the command had slid by them, too. Roehm spared them a fast glance, then did a double take. "Shift!" he ordered and punched out even harder with his alpha power. Nothing happened.

"I'm sorry," said Guivre coolly, "but we don't allow uninvited gatecrashers to operate significant magic in our town." She didn't sound the least bit apologetic.

Before anyone could react, Roehm pulled out a huge handgun and aimed it straight at Jackie's chest. "Then I'll just kill her now and take back what she stole."

Trevor shoved her behind him and let out an inhumanly loud growl. She wrapped her arms around his waist, willing him to listen. "Stay human. He wants you outside our circle. The bullets are animal poison."

"Pendragor, if you would be so kind?" Guivre sounded like she was asking someone to pour tea.

Jackie felt rather than saw the power of the wand that the amethyst-eyed fairy had wielded earlier. Roehm yowled in pain. She peeked around Trevor in time to see a puddle of molten metal burning a hole in the tarp. Roehm stumbled away toward the far edge, holding his charred hand to his chest, yowling. He fumbled at his neckline.

Jackie slid herself around Trevor to stand in front of him and sent her magical senses out to see what Roehm was reaching for. "Roehm's got a lightning charm," she shouted.

Pendragor's eyes narrowed as he wielded his slender wand like he was conducting an orchestra. Power surged. Roehm's screaming turned to screeches of agony as five places on his clothes burst into unnatural green flame, then exploded with fireworks. He twirled in a mad dance, trying to get away from the sparks.

"Oh, do cease the melodrama, Alpha Roehm." Guivre's

expression was neutral, but her tone was peevish. "We all know your burns will heal in minutes."

Instead of answering, Roehm launched himself toward Jackie, tearing out of his clothes in a half-shift to give himself muscles, claws, and teeth. Even as she dropped to the ground in a ball to protect herself and her child, Trevor full-shifted in a heartbeat and launched out of the chalk circle to meet Roehm head-on.

Roehm's body bounced off Trevor's huge bear as if he'd hit a wall. He rolled away and finished shifting, but the enraged bear was right there with twenty-inch claws that ripped into the lion's soft underbelly.

The lion scrambled up and leapt onto the much larger bear's back, biting down and sinking claws into the bear's heavily shaggy fur. The bear stood upright and shook, throwing the lion off. In a blur of motion, the bear spun and dropped his front body weight, landing heavy paws on the lion's back. Everyone heard the sickening crack as the lion's spine snapped.

Incredibly, the lion pulled itself around using its front paws and sank sharp teeth into the meaty part of the bear's back leg. The bear turned and bit the lion's flattened ear, but the lion clamped its jaws tighter. The bear tried again, but only succeeded in dragging the lion's weight around in a circle.

Jackie remembered a tactic from one of the many fights she'd seen on Roehm's compound. She rolled and sat up. "Trevor," she shouted, "your human leg is smaller!"

The bear made a throaty sound and became a man in jeans. Before the surprised lion could react, Trevor pried the lion's jaws open enough to free his bleeding thigh. Trevor limped backward, never taking his eyes off the lion.

"Do what you did to the coyotes," she yelled.

Trevor nodded, then shot a questioning glance toward Guivre. The golden elf nodded. Trevor squared his shoulders and turned to stare at Roehm.

Everyone with any magical senses at all felt the full, raw strength of Trevor's alpha command. As before in the alley, it washed over and through her like a soothing wave and had no effect on her unborn daughter.

Roehm fought the command with his own alpha power, but in less than fifteen seconds, he was nakedly human and lying on the tarp, legs inert, and bleeding from four lacerations on his stomach.

"Fine," croaked Roehm, "you can have the skank." His voice was weaker than she'd ever heard it. "But everything she has, she stole from us, and we want it back." He growled as he raised himself up on his elbows. "She has to pay for what she did to Ruben."

Jackie awkwardly climbed to her feet and brushed the dust off her pants. She looked at Roehm's pride members, who were showing varying degrees of fear and disbelief. They'd never seen Roehm bested at anything. They looked just like the board of one of her megachurch clients when she'd told them they'd been conned by their minister in a Ponzi scheme. Some of them refused to believe it, even when the minister and his wife pled guilty and were sentenced to a dozen years in prison.

Jackie put one foot on the tarp and raised her hand, uncertain of the protocol. "Uhm, excuse me? Am I allowed to tell my side?" Thanks to the elven magic, her soft voice carried.

Roehm's right leg twitched, meaning his shifter healing was already repairing his spine and nervous system. "Are you going to take the word of a human?" He made it sound like she was mess to be scraped off his boots.

Jackie was used to it, but she was tired of it. Tired of being hated for the color of her skin, or her gender, or her magic, or her achievements, or her humanity. She'd been guilty of prejudice, too, in thinking Barry Wills, a lying leopard, and Roehm, a twisted sociopath lion, were typical shifters. The young lynx-shifter guards looked out for each other and some of the others against Roehm. She'd seen compassion and caring in the rough-around-the edges coyotes, and Trevor... she wanted to hitch her wagon to his star and follow him wherever he wanted to go. Preferably the nearest bed.

She waved to get the attention of the wand-wielding fairy, who casually leaned against the council's table. "Master Pendragor, compel me to tell the truth and ask me what happened and what I stole." She put her hands protectively over her stomach. "As long as it won't hurt my child."

Guivre glided around the table and onto the tarp, taking in the crowd with a sweep of her eyes. Her gaze lingered on Roehm's pride and Roehm himself, before finally lighting on Jackie with a long, assessing look. "It shall be as you have asked. I suspect this tale needs a more comfortable setting."

"If we don't invite Florinel Brooker to observe," said Pendragor, deftly twirling his now shiny wand like it was a miniature cheerleader's baton, "we'll never hear the end of it."

Guivre looked annoyed, then sighed. "You're right, of course." She waved a finger toward Roehm. "Besides, he will need time to heal and collect his pride."

Jackie cleared her throat. "Sorry if I'm out of line again, but could someone look at Trevor's leg?" Blood had thoroughly soaked the leg of his jeans. She wished she had one of her mother's magical healing poultices in her back pocket. If he was anything like the felines in the pride, he'd heal the battle wounds in a day, but it would be less painful if the lacerations were clean.

Trevor waved off her concern. "I'll be fine." He glanced at Pendragor, then turned and nodded respectfully at Guivre. "Can Jackie and her child get sanctuary, or at least a guest invitation until the hearing?"

Guivre crossed to behind the table to hold a whispered conversation with the council members.

Pendragor sat casually on the edge of the table and whistled. The seemingly careless tune had subtle power in every note. In other circumstances, Jackie would have loved to ask what the magic did.

Roehm began dragging himself along the tarp, toward his pride. Jackie felt the telepathic command he sent to his enforcers. Two cougars stepped onto the tarp and lifted him by his shoulders. Jackie had never been able to hear his orders. She'd assumed it was because she wasn't a true member of the pride, but maybe her humanity got in the way. Not that she wanted to listen to anything Roehm had to say, but maybe it meant she wouldn't be a good mate for Trevor.

The thought stunned her. Was she really thinking of mating with him? Surely, she just had a case of animal... okay, shifter lust. And there would be no lust-indulging that night, not with Trevor's leg still healing.

Her back hurt, and the brim of her borrowed ball cap dripped with sweat. She felt like a tiny paper boat caught in the middle of a fast-running river. She was determined to do what was best for her daughter, but now she had Trevor to worry about, too.

Trevor glanced at the whispering council members, then limped toward her. The second he stepped into the chalk circle, she wrapped him in her arms. She drew in the scent and warmth of him while she could.

He seemed to sense her worry, and gently cradled her head against his chest. "We'll be okay," he murmured, then kissed her forehead. "Really."

"Maybe." She pulled back to look at the man who was becoming the center of her dreams and fantasies. "You humiliated Roehm. Now he wants to kill you, too."

"Yeah, but it was worth it." The corners of his mouth twitched with a smile. "Thanks for the coaching, Alpha Fight Master."

Jackie rolled her eyes. "I'm serious. When they were handing out honor, Roehm was sneaking in the back window, stealing extra helpings of greed and treachery."

Trevor drew breath to speak, but was interrupted by Guivre clearing her throat.

"The council grants permanent sanctuary to Trevor Hammond, should he still wish it. The council grants temporary sanctuary to Jacqueline Breton and her child, with full glade protection." Guivre's dry recitation gave no hint of her personal opinion in the matter. She turned to meet Pendragor's eyes with a long, meaningful look. Telepathy, Jackie guessed.

The lavender-skinned fairy nodded, then stood up from his slouch and turned sharp eyes to a scowling Roehm. Two of his guards were holding him up since his legs still didn't work.

"Alpha Roehm, these are the terms. Six days from now, at noon, the full town council will hear your claim against Jacqueline Breton. We will grant passage for you and your pride on that day, but none of you may stay on our lands in the interim."

One of Roehm's enforcers growled that he'd stay

wherever he wanted, but another elbowed him sharply and pointed to the sky, where the afternoon sun blazed through wispy clouds. "They have dragons, you moron."

Pendragor smiled without humor. "We do, indeed."

"Six days is too long," growled Roehm. "She could find some human hidey-hole and disappear."

Jackie found herself the center of attention. She started to speak, then remembered to put a foot on the tarp so she could be heard. "Six days is fine with me. I promise I'll stay." She crossed her arms.

Before Roehm could react, Pendragor pointed his wand at her foot, and power surged. "Your word is your bond." An invisible weight settled around her ankle. It felt like a tracking spell. She nodded and stepped back. Trevor moved to stand behind her and rest his hands on her shoulders.

A crafty look passed over Roehm's face. "I demand you impound everything she's got. It's evidence."

Jackie sent a disdainful look toward Roehm's naked, filthy, slack body. "I don't think my maternity pants will fit you."

Trevor snorted behind her, and the crowd laughed. Even the wyvern chuckled.

"I think not," said Guivre, with a small smile. She waved fingers in obvious dismissal. "Leave within the hour or feed our dragons. Come back in six days or forfeit." Her tone said she didn't care one way or the other.

She turned her back on him and walked back around the table toward the wyvern. "Scholar, a word?"

Roehm swore a blue streak as his guards turned with him and headed toward the haphazard circle of decidedly worse-for-wear vehicles. Jackie felt sorry for the members of his pride, because once he healed, they'd likely be his punching bags.

Pendragor crossed toward Jackie and Trevor. As he did so, he pointed his wand toward the tarp and whistled three notes. The magic vanished so suddenly it made Jackie's ears pop.

Up close, Pendragor seemed both more and less human. His flowing poet's shirt revealed a chiseled, toned chest, worthy of being a cover model, but his variegated purple and gold hair turned out to be very fine feathers, and his eyes had an avian shape. She had never seen a fairy like him.

He waved toward her ankle, where the tracking spell still tingled. "You may go anywhere in the glade. I'll introduce you to Shiloh, the deputy sheriff, so he can look out for you." She thought she heard hints of a Russian accent in his musical voice. He gave her a wide smile. "You'll like him."

Behind her, Trevor rumbled, then coughed.

Pendragor laughed and looked up at Trevor. "You'll like him, too. He's very happily mated."

She turned to look at Trevor in time to catch him blushing. She had to admit to being secretly flattered he was jealous and trying to hide it. Outside of the shifter-mate potential thing, men had rarely been interested in her for more than a casual good time, and she didn't do casual.

"Mr. Hammond," said Pendragor, "I am pleased to welcome you to Kotoyeesinay. The glade's border will be instructed to admit you." His tone sounded more formal than before.

"Call me Trevor. Glad to be here, and thanks. That magic barrier packs a whallop." He squeezed her shoulders briefly. "I forgot to warn Jackie about it."

Jackie shuddered at the memory. "Felt like being strapped naked to an exam table."

"Apologies." Pendragor shook his head. "The border was

fine until they built the casino. Their security team added a complex set of spells to let the tourists in, and discourage the rest, while letting magical people and those in need in, but warn us about those with ill intent. It's been a mess ever since. I'm trying to get it fixed."

From out of a pocket that his form-fitting black pants should have been entirely too tight to have, Pendragor produced what looked like a tree-shaped trinket on a keychain and held it out to Trevor. "This charm is for your truck, so you can access the shortcut to town. I think you could find load-hauling customers here."

Trevor smiled as he took the keychain. "That will definitely come in handy."

Jackie realized she'd completely and selfishly forgotten that Trevor had upended his life and business just to bring her to safety. She turned to face him. "You need to get your trailer in Nebraska and deliver your load of furniture. Billings, wasn't it?"

A stubborn look settled on his face. "I'm not leaving until the hearing."

She crossed her arms and gave him her best stubborn look back. "Oh, yes, you are. I'm safe here until then, and it's bad for your bottom line to piss off your customers."

"It's my..." He trailed off, then blew out a noisy breath. A flurry of emotions flitted across his face, too fast for her to read them. "You're right. But I'm not leaving until I meet this sheriff guy, and not at all if I don't trust him."

She nodded. "Deal." She reached out and took his hand, lacing her fingers through his, then turned to Pendragor. "Would you please introduce us to Deputy Sheriff Shiloh?"

6

The hardest thing Trevor had ever done in his life was leave Jackie in Kotoyeesinay. It helped that Deputy Sheriff Shiloh, a coyote shifter with permanently pointed teeth, turned out to be competent, garrulous, and true-mated to a suave jaguar shifter named Matteo. Despite her multiple assurances that she would be fine, he didn't like it. His bear shredded him from the inside for not staying to protect her.

He used his shifter strength to stay awake in the night and make record time to Nebraska. Along the way, he faced up to his own fears that she wouldn't be there when he got back. To be brutally honest with himself, he had precious little to offer her, not even a home to share. Despite their white-hot attraction, she didn't feel the mate bond the way he did. She also had a baby to worry about.

Some of that he could remedy. He went over on his cellular phone minutes to call her each night. The sound of her voice and her amusement with the quirky residents of Kotoyeesinay helped keep him sane. He called in favors and made arrangements that would help Jackie and her child, even if she closed her heart to him for being just another shifter who might hurt her. He'd promised he'd do everything so Jackie could keep her daughter, and he planned to deliver.

The morning of the sixth day found him trying to break land speed records for a big rig, barreling hot through the Kotoyeesinay border and racing into town to the high school, where the hearing would be held.

He spotted her immediately, waiting for him in the shade of the roof's overhang at the loading dock, where she'd arranged for him to park his truck. The need to touch and smell her had him scrambling out of his cab and into her open arms.

"I missed you." He nuzzled into her neck and drew in the scent of her. His sour, grumpy bear sighed inside him with pleasure.

"Right back at you, cowboy." She sighed and tightened her arms around his waist.

He nibbled his way along her jaw until he found her lips and lost himself in the taste of her. He slid his hands down to rhythmically caress the beautiful globes of her butt.

She surfaced for air and backed up a little. "Much as I want more of this," she said, palming the side of his face, "we shouldn't give the kids something to try at home, if you catch my drift."

Her radiant smile made him want to lick every inch of her, but he definitely didn't want an audience for that.

He belatedly noticed she was wearing a nice jacket and blouse, and his nuzzling had mussed part of her contained hairstyle. He straightened her jacket and smoothed down her springy hair with his thumb. "Sorry."

She laughed. "I'll fix it when we go in." She pointed toward the propped-open side door. "Shiloh is waiting to show us to the gym instead of the auditorium, because apparently"—she rolled her eyes—"everyone in Kotoyeesinay is in there."

"What about Roehm?"

She nodded. "Shiloh said Roehm called up the rest of the pride, so the council had to give them a section of the bleachers."

"The dude doesn't do subtle, does he?" He made a rude sound. "Asshole."

"And then some," agreed Jackie. "Let's go in. We've got a few minutes before the hearing starts, and I have news."

She led him to a small classroom that had been set aside for them. The only decent places to sit were the teacher's desk and chair. Trevor took the chair, then pulled her willingly into his lap. He didn't even care if she noticed his body's ready response to her when she settled against his chest.

"News?" he asked, to distract himself from the temptation to start something they definitely couldn't finish in a rolling chair.

"Shiloh's mate, Matteo, isn't just a lawyer, he's a high-rate corporate lawyer on retainer to the Shifter Tribunal. He tracked down my ex. His real name is Barry Williken, of the Hamptons Willikens. Very old shifter pride, very rich, very conservative. Barry is the son of the pride leader. They have marriage alliance plans for him that don't include humans."

Trevor frowned. "What about you and your daughter?"

"Matteo got Barry and the pride to sign a blood oath give up any and all claims to me or Princess." She smiled. "Seems Barry was supposed to be lying low in Houston, not knocking up his human girlfriend and losing big in Las Vegas. According to Matteo, the scandal would have shattered the business deal. Oh, excuse me, the wedding."

"Would you have wanted to be a Williken?" He failed to quash the thread of fear that he couldn't measure up to a rich, powerful family.

"Hell, no." She gave an exaggerated shudder. "Shoot me now."

He laughed and tightened his hold on her. "Congratulations, then."

Shiloh poked his head in. "Showtime."

Jackie slid off his lap to stand. "Let's get this over with. I want to move onto the next chapter of my lifebook." She picked up a messenger bag and slung it on her shoulder.

After a stop at the restroom, and just before they entered the gym, he pulled Jackie into a long hug. He meant it to be reassuring, to tell her he'd always be in her corner, but her fantastic scent and the feel of her skin on his again woke up his ever-hopeful dick, leaving him hard and wanting. He tried to hide it from her, but she'd laughed and kissed him hard and fast. "Save those naughty thoughts, darlin'." Her whispered Texas drawl made his full-blown erection throb.

Just how he wanted to walk in and be seen by the entire frickin' town.

On the way in, Shiloh pointed out the witness area, which was ordinarily the basketball free-throw zone painted on the gym floor. Once again, magic made it possible for everyone to hear anything said in the witness box.

The town council, seated at long tables, was now twelve. Guivre Gul-Vert, in a dress made of deep red and white flowers, presided. New faces included a dark elf who specialized in the study of magic and a pale, terrifying-looking gothic wraith with an incongruously warm smile. Shiloh mentioned their names, but Trevor couldn't remember names of people he couldn't smell unless he wrote them down.

The area set aside for Jackie to wait was behind a defensive magic perimeter, designated by orange hazard cones. He held the folding chair steady, so Jackie could sit, then sat in the one beside her. He threaded his fingers through hers and rested their joined hands on her thigh. She glanced at Roehm and the front row of his crew, then focused on the council. Her serene outward appearance belied the tension he felt in her. He squeezed her fingers gently.

For his part, Trevor counted over forty pride members in the roped-off bleacher section, then studied Roehm and his half-naked enforcers with a careful eye, especially the ten crammed into three rows in Roehm's waiting area. Trevor had several permanent scars from his younger, wilder days, when he'd naively underestimated his opponents. Just because he didn't see any weapons didn't mean they weren't carrying.

Deputy Shiloh stood to Jackie's left, his thumbs tucked into his utility belt. He gave them a knowing wink, then settled his face into a neutral expression.

At fifteen minutes after noon, Roehm stood and began pacing, once again healthy and looking twice as pissed off as he had before.

Trevor had never wanted to kill anyone before, but he'd make an exception for Roehm. During their final dominance battle, Trevor had taken the measure of the shifter and found him corrosively corrupt. He gave alphas a bad name, surrounding himself with the weak and damaged, and making them worse.

Trevor took a deep breath and let it out slowly. He'd learned the hard way he couldn't fix everything, and patience worked in unexpected ways.

Four bell-like chimes sounded, and the room quieted.

Pendragor, the fairy with the wand, and dressed in lime-colored corset-vest over a dark tunic, and thigh-high boots, explained the rules for the hearing, including the prohibition of unauthorized magic. Jackie would speak first, and everyone else should sit down and keep quiet, or else. He looked pointedly at Roehm. It took a long moment for Roehm to realize that meant him, too. He sat, legs sprawled in front of him, arms crossed, and glared at anyone who caught his eye.

Pendragor invited Jackie into the witness box. "Consent for a geas spell of truth speaking?"

Jackie nodded.

Pendragor sketched a movement with his wand. Trevor felt the power of it as a thrumming against his chest.

It suddenly hit Trevor why she was willing to undergo the truth spell, even though the unpleasant facts might open her to other charges. She'd trapped Roehm into either submitting to the spell and being condemned by the truth, or refusing the spell, and being condemned by his own lies.

That was it. He loved her.

He'd already been half in love with her by the time he'd held her in his arms and promised to help her keep her child. His heart swelled when she'd helped him keep his head in the fight. But smart, clever women had always been his honey, and she had that in abundance.

The woman he was in love with sat with her bag in her lap, proud and brave, in the center of the witness box. She told her story.

When she got to the part about finding the secret accounting ledger, she pulled a slim black-and-red journal out of her bag and gave it to Pendragor.

Roehm jumped to his feet with a loud verbal barrage,

claiming she didn't know what she was talking about, they were confidential, she forged them, and they weren't his.

Tiny golden elf Guivre frowned and gestured with two fingers. "Sit down." His chair slammed into the back of his knees, forcing him to fall back into it. The chair slid back into its place. Roehm snarled and struggled to stand again but seemed to be fighting invisible shackles.

Jackie's lips tightened in annoyance. "I'm a certified public accountant with criminal forensics experience. I know a ledger when I see one." She nailed Roehm with her gaze. "Alpha Roehm has been skimming seventy to eighty percent of the pride's gross income from stolen cars, and illegal gun and drug sales, then taking his 'lion's share' of the puny profit he reported to the pride in the spreadsheet program on his personal computer." She turned her attention to several of the pride who'd been allowed to sit behind Roehm in chairs on the gymnasium floor. "Ask the Shifter Tribunal for an outside audit if you don't believe..." Her words trailed off, and she paled.

Trevor focused his predator's gaze on the pride members, wondering what had shaken her. The lynx-shifter enforcers sat together like the juvenile delinquents they obviously were. The jaguar looked pissed off. The sad cheetah shifter stared at his feet. An obese leopard shifter sat uncomfortably on a chair that was too small for his fat ass. The scarecrow-skinny leopard shifter next to him yawned and scratched under the kerchief at his neck, revealing a recent, still-unhealed scar.

Realization slammed into Trevor. He was looking at Ricardo, the obese leopard shifter who'd planned to sell Jackie's baby at auction, and Ruben, the skinny leopard shifter who she thought she'd killed. Who was obviously very much alive.

Trevor ruthlessly sat on his bear to keep from whining and distracting Jackie even more. He didn't know what else to do but pump every bit of love he had into the thin mate bond that was growing between them, and hope she'd feel it and draw strength from it.

Jackie straightened her shoulders. "I admit I stole from the pride. They already took back the motorcycle with their harpoon, and I will gladly return everything that's left." She gave Roehm a sharp smile that had nothing to do with humor. "Especially the ledger."

"What about the money we paid for you?" demanded skinny Ruben. "We bought you food and fat-girl clothes, too. And what about the money for that illegal shifter child you're carrying?"

Ricardo elbowed Ruben hard. "Shut up, you moron."

"No, you shut up." Ruben elbowed Ricardo back. "We're out twenty thousand for a worthless skank."

Jackie's harsh laugh cut them off. "Check the ledger. Roehm only paid fifteen thousand for all six of us he bought from the auction and pocketed the rest."

A large, well-dressed man with brown skin and long, straight black hair rose from the first row of the bleachers and stepped into the witness area. Trevor's bear nose told him the man was a shifter, but of unknown species. "Who is the father of the leopard child you're carrying? Does he know where you are?"

"Who are you?" asked Jackie. She seemed calm, but her fingers knotted together in her lap.

The man frowned. "I am Florinel Brooker, and a member of the Shifter Tribunal. Answer the question." He oozed authority.

Jackie jutted her chin out. "No. It's not germane."

Trevor stood and drilled Brooker with a warning look. Brooker frowned and opened his mouth to speak.

Guivre's voice interrupted. "Enough, Mr. Brooker." A core of iron underpinned her golden-soft tone. "We invited you out of courtesy to your Tribunal. You have no jurisdiction in sanctuary decisions."

Brooker's expression stilled. After a moment, he gave a curt nod, then returned to his seat.

Trevor turned to catch Jackie's eye. He nodded to tell her he'd always be there for her, then sat down again.

Guivre rose from her chair and crossed to Jackie. For the first time since they'd arrived, and all the events of the afternoon, Guivre's expression bordered on sympathetic as she looked at Jackie. "We will not compel you to speak of how you became pregnant. However, if we grant you sanctuary, you may never be able to leave Kotoyeesinay again."

Jackie flicked a glance toward Brooker, then back to Guivre. "If the Tribunal takes my child away, what will happen to her?"

Guivre rocked back on her heels, a shocked look on her face. "I was under the impression the Tribunal stopped that centuries ago." Her lips thinned as she turned a frosty gaze on Brooker. "Am I wrong?"

Brooker shook his head, clearly appalled. "We don't take away children." He shot a narrow-eyed, speculative glance at Roehm.

Guivre turned back to Jackie. "The choice is yours."

Jackie looked to Trevor. Damn, he wished they'd had more time to talk. He tried to convey without words that he would love her feline child as much as he already loved her. That was part of the magic of shifter mates.

Jackie closed her eyes for a long moment, then sighed

and opened them. "The father of my child is a leopard shifter named Barry Williken. He claimed I was his mate." Tears welled up in her eyes. "When I accidentally became pregnant, he sold me to an auction house in Las Vegas because I have shifter-mate potential. That's why Roehm bought me for his pride. They were going to sell my baby, then force-change me so I could breed again." She wiped away the tear that fell and caught Trevor's gaze with her own. "Barry wasn't my mate. I know that now, after having met Trevor."

Trevor crossed to her and knelt by her side. He held his hand out to her in invitation. She put her hand in his, and he pulled it close, so he could rest his face against her palm. "I love you, Jacqueline Breton. And Princess, too." His words boomed throughout the gym, but he didn't care. He'd shout it from the mountaintops if he had to.

She smiled at him and used her thumb to brush the tear that fell down his cheek. "I love you, Trevor Hammond." She put her hand on her stomach. "We love you."

He kissed the back of her hand. "Marry me."

She laughed, though it sounded wet from her tears. "Of course, I'll marry you. I can't tell a lie: You're my mate."

The tenuous bond between them strengthened and widened. She was without a doubt the most remarkable woman in the universe, and he hoped he could give her everything she deserved.

Noise impinged on the little world that held only him and the mate he would love the rest of his life. It sounded like... cheering?

He looked around and saw the people in the bleachers standing and clapping. Some whistled, and others stomped. He saw happy faces as wet with tears as his and his mate's.

Closer movement drew his attention. Brooker dragged a

struggling Roehm to Pendragor, who was still holding the ledger book, and demanded a truth spell so he could get details. A host of djinn guards surrounded Roehm's pride, but only dimwitted Ruben tried to get past them, and nearly lost an ear for his trouble.

"Ow!" Jackie put her hand on her stomach.

Trevor gave her an alarmed look. He suddenly realized he didn't know anything about pregnant women, or babies, or even how to change a diaper. Babies needed cribs. Leopards needed trees to climb. Houses needed beds and flowers and curtains...

Jackie took his face in her hands. "Don't panic. I'm fine. That's just Princess, giving me the elbow, letting me know she's still here. We'll figure this out together."

"I don't have anything to give you," he admitted. "My parents' clan kicked me out because I'm not like them. I only have my truck."

"Silly bear." She leaned over and kissed his nose. "As long as we have each other, everything else is gravy."

The loudest, longest whistle Trevor ever heard in his life had everyone in the gym holding their hands over their ears or covering their heads with their paws. Even the wyvern tried to bury its head under its wing.

Guivre waved delicate fingers, and the noise stopped. "Thank you."

The only sound in the room was the air conditioning as she glided to the table where the council sat and faced them. She spoke to them in a language Trevor didn't recognize. After a moment, most of them nodded.

She turned to face Trevor and Jackie. "Full sanctuary is granted to Jacqueline Breton and her child."

Pandemonium erupted in the room, making it impossible to talk. Trevor pumped fists into the air and roared his happiness, then folded Jackie in a tight embrace and kissed her soundly. She kissed him right back, then said something he couldn't hear.

"I love you, too." That was safe, right?

She laughed and pulled his head toward hers, so she could yell in his ear.

"I need to pee!"

He laughed as he scooped her up into his arms and started carrying her toward the double doors. If his mate needed a bathroom, that's what she'd get. And anything else it was his power to give.

7

Jackie's fervent desire to be alone with her mate after the hearing was frustrated by a request from Brooker to tell him what she could about the auction.

Then she had to talk Trevor into letting her go without him, because he'd promised to defend her and her baby from the Shifter Tribunal. "I love you, but you can't protect me from the past or my memories. The sooner they know, the sooner they can act." She gave him a long kiss that left them both panting, then handed him the key to her room. "If you buy enough food for us, we won't have to leave the motel for days. I'll be there as soon as I'm done with Brooker."

She'd set the meeting at the sheriff's station just in case she needed backup. Despite the confidence she'd shown to Trevor, she wasn't one-hundred-percent convinced the Shifter Tribunal wouldn't try to steamroll her because she was a human who would soon be raising a leopard shifter daughter.

Deputy Shiloh showed them to an empty office that

belonged to the vacationing sheriff and left them alone. She sat in one of the two visitor chairs and put her bottle of water on the big mahogany desk. Brooker sat in the other, then set a small tape recorder on the desk. It had the subtle feel of talisman magic.

Seen up close, Brooker was younger than she'd thought, though it was hard to tell with shifters. He had impressively wide shoulders and was handsome enough to be a movie star.

He waved toward the tape recorder. "This is spelled to transcribe and transmit what we say to the enforcement office in Chicago. But first, I owe you an apology for asking about the father of your child."

She tilted her head. "You do?"

"We had a case last year. A wizard recruited human women with shifter-mate potential to have sex with shifters, paid a witch to ensure they got pregnant, then blackmailed the fathers. Some of the women knew exactly what they were getting into and went along with it for the money." His lips curved downward in a thin, tight frown. "I let my suspicion runaway with my good sense. In short, I fucked up, and I'm sorry."

"Forgiven." Empathy rose in her, and she sighed. "It's hard, facing up to your own prejudices. I wouldn't be with Trevor if I hadn't faced up to mine." She pointed her chin toward the small, shield-shaped gold pin on his lapel. "Besides, you're in a lonely business, where you only see people at their worst. I couldn't do police work if my life depended on it."

"Thank you." After a moment, he reached out to turn on the tape recorder, but she stopped him.

"What are you going to do with Roehm and his pride?"

"Arrange to have them ported to holding cells in

Chicago." He smiled reassuringly. "They won't be anywhere near you for a long time."

"That's good to know, but I'd like to ask that you look at the pride members as individuals and see if they can be... rehabilitated, I guess. Find new prides or clans for them." She pulled the bottle of water off the desk and held it on her stomach. "A few are just as bad as Roehm, but most are Roehm's victims, not his supporters. The young lynx brothers are orphans who don't know anything else. The cheetah mourns his dead mate, who he thinks he killed, when it was actually Roehm who did it. I bet the compound still has the tiger guard in the garage, chained with magic so he can't shift, and starved so he'll eat anything he can catch."

She took a deep breath and shook herself, to keep the tears at bay. "Most were hurting, damaged, just trying to get by, looking for the safety of the pride, hoping the leader would help them. Instead, they got a got a greedy sociopath who fed on them, worse than any blood-mad vampire."

Brooker's expression went flat, which she suspected meant she'd surprised him. After several long moments, he nodded. "I can't speak for the Tribunal regarding what will happen to Roehm, but what you're asking is the right thing to do." A corner of his mouth twitched with what may have been a smile. "I'll assign it myself, so I know it's done right."

She pointed to the tape recorder. "So, speaking of greedy sociopaths who run auction houses in the basement of a Las Vegas hotel..."

The afternoon sun kissed the western horizon as Jackie walked from the sheriff's station to the motel. It had taken her a lot longer than she'd expected to tell Brooker her story and answer his questions, and now she was horny and hungry. She could have asked for a ride, but nothing was far in Kotoyeesinay, she needed time to think about what she wanted to say to Trevor. Her fiancé. Her goddess-gifted true mate. The man she loved.

They were both strong, independent personalities, so their marriage would founder if it wasn't an equal partnership. She'd immediately regretted sending him away after the fight with Roehm, and missed him every moment while he was gone, but she didn't want him sacrificing his business for her. It would have been a poor start to what she hoped was a long and successful union.

She'd ruthlessly quizzed Shiloh and Matteo about all things shifter. To her vast relief, they told her that once she and Trevor mated, her scent would change, so she'd no longer be a sex magnet to horny shifters. As Matteo described it, the mate bond would be plain as daylight to any shifter, and they'd both smell boringly off-limits. They'd also assured her shifters could easily form a mate bond with a human, especially one like her with her own magic.

With mating in mind, and her body totally on board for the thrill ride, she let herself into the motel room, only to find Trevor not there. No brown and gold big rig in the parking lot, either, or on a nearby street. Princess kicked, just like Jackie wanted to. She rubbed her belly. "You and me both, baby."

To kill time, she changed into a T-shirt with a picture of the death star over her round belly and stretch maternity pants with a wide, soft waistband, then hung up the outfit she'd worn to the hearing.

During the week, she'd been astonished at how many townspeople had gone out of their way to welcome her, convinced she'd be granted sanctuary. Trevor had left her all the cash he had, but hardly anyone would take her money. The motel room was free because of a called-in favor from Shiloh and Matteo. The diners and restaurants said her meals were on the house. The owner of a clothing store outright gave her some fun maternity clothes, including the business suit she wore for the hearing. Not even Shepherd, Trevor's seven-foot-tall ogre mechanic friend, would let her pay for the motorcycle repairs.

At first, she'd been perturbed. When she was coming up, she and her mother had sometimes made do with bread soup, but they weren't charity cases. It had taken her several days to realize that the town's generosity had no strings—no return obligation, no sneering condescension. It was the kind of community she'd always dreamed of but had never found. She really wanted to stay, but that was on the long list of things to discuss with Trevor. He had a say in that, too.

No sense sitting around, waiting for a man who'd apparently gone all the way to Laramie to shop for food, so she spread out her wardrobe on the bed.

Outside of the business outfit, her clothes were highly inappropriate for a wedding. Cheap maternity pants and tops in dreadful colors, second-hand work shirts, a pair of slip-on canvas shoes, two of Trevor's T-shirts for sleeping in, and her motorcycle riding gear. If Trevor wouldn't go for a quick visit to the Justice of the Peace, maybe she could talk him into a sky clad wedding, like her Wiccan friends had in Houston. She'd rather be naked than look like a something the cat dragged in. She folded and rolled up her clothes and returned them to her backpack in the closet. The drawers in the motel room's dresser smelled like spilled perfume, which her newly sensitive nose couldn't abide.

She flung herself into the stuffed chair. Her empty stomach suggested pizza. She couldn't go anywhere, because that would guarantee he'd come back to find *her* gone and go out looking. She realized it wasn't fair to have expected him to sit around waiting for her, either.

A sudden swell of doubt washed over her. Was he having second thoughts about marrying a human? Did he hate the idea of living in a house instead of his truck? Did he think she was too emotional or too clingy? Did it bother him that she was nine years younger? She stood up and gave herself a mental shake while arching her back in a stretch. It was likely the pregnancy hormones, magnifying her feelings and warping her rational brain.

Princess elbowed her, reminding her not to mope. She had a feeling her daughter was going to be more interested in martial arts than ballet.

Which meant she needed a job, because martial arts clothes—and shifter obstetricians—weren't free, and she damn sure wasn't going to make Trevor pay for everything. Besides, she wasn't cut out to be idle.

She had debts to pay and food to buy, soon for two. A wedding dress to buy. Now that she had transportation again, she could apply for any position in town, but she needed a job she could do from home for a while. Too bad she didn't have something like Brooker's cassette recorder with its magical ability to transmit to Chicago from wherever he was. Maybe she could figure out how to do it with computerized spreadsheets.

Inspired, she called Matteo's office, and the receptionist put her right through. "Does the Shifter Tribunal need an accountant?"

8

Trevor was pretty sure his mate was going to kill him for being so late. He'd wanted everything to be perfect, and time had gotten away from him.

Just as he approached the motel room door, he heard her asking about a job with the Shifter Tribunal.

He awkwardly unlocked the door and opened it, then sidestepped in with his bags.

Jackie turned, her eyes growing wide. "Good. I'll bring you a résumé on Monday. Gotta go." She hung up the phone. "What did you do, buy out the store?" She smiled, and he relaxed a bit. "Oh, never mind. I'm glad you're back." She crossed to the dresser that held a TV, a coffee maker, and a hot plate. "Here, put them in the kitchen."

He set them all down, then arranged them so they wouldn't spill. "I've got another load."

"I'll help, because we need to talk."

As they brought in the rest of the bags and his large cooler, he admitted he might have gone overboard with the supplies. He tried not to let her words worry him, but he didn't do a very good job.

He sat on the corner of the bed and braced himself for bad news. "You wanted to talk."

She crossed to stand in front of him. "I'm on the pregnancy roller coaster right now, and all I can think about is the Moon pies you brought and jumping your bones." She put a hand on his shoulder. "Are you sure you want to mate with me? I know it's for life, and I want that, but you have to be sure, too." She slid her other hand over her stomach.

Relief flooded him. "Damn sure. I want you forever. Mating means your daughter becomes the daughter of my heart, and I want that, too." He placed a gentle hand over hers on her stomach. "Some shifters never get the chance to meet their true mate, and not all matings are blessed with children. I hit the jackpot with you."

She gave him a radiant smile, so he didn't mind the tears. He patted the bed next to him. "I have a question for you."

She sat, and he put an arm around her to snuggle her close.

"Do you want to move to Chicago?" It would throw half his arrangements out the window, but he'd do it in a heartbeat if that's where her job was. His job was mobile, but his home base would always be with her.

"No. I'd like to live here." Her eyes filled with more tears. "I've made more friends here in a week than I did in four years living in Houston." She captured his hand and kissed his palm. "How does claiming work? Shiloh and Matteo said it creates the bond, but they got all coy about the details, so I assume it's sex." She used her sleeve to wipe the tears from her face. "Goddess, I hope it's sex."

"Oh, yeah." Trevor pulled her in for a kiss, licking at the seam of her lips until she opened for him. The feel and taste of her set him on fire. "Hot, raunchy sex with enthusiastic intent."

She stood up to strip the T-shirt off over her head and threw it on the stuffed chair. She started on her bra. "Well then, get undressed, cowboy," she drawled. "I've been wanting you real bad for a whole week."

He flared his magic to do the one trick he knew, vanishing his clothes until he called for them again. He watched, mesmerized as she pushed off her pants and underwear. Yellow light from the bedside lamp lit her large, beautiful breasts and swelling stomach, like she'd been painted by a master artist. He wasted no time in pulling her to him, so he could latch onto one proud, taut nipple. She moaned as he swirled his tongue around it and sucked gently, then repeated the cycle. He did the same for her other breast, reveling in her pleasure.

"Bed," she whispered.

He scooped her up and stood, kissing her wetly before laying her on her back on top of the covers of the king-size bed. Her smile widened when her eyes drifted down and centered on his erection. Her anticipation flowed through the nascent mate bond, causing him to pulse with need.

He knelt on the bed and stalked her on his hands and knees until he got to her splayed thighs. The scent of her arousal drew him like the finest honey. He lowered his head to the center of her curls for a taste.

"Oh, goddess, yes, do that again." She clutched the sheets. "More."

He ran his hands up her thighs and slid them under her generous ass, then gave his mate what she asked for. He licked his way through her folds until he found her swollen clit, which he flicked several times with his tongue until he found the angle that had her thrusting her hips and gasping his name.

He swirled down into her well for more of her honey,

curling his tongue into her to get it all. Her muscles tightened around him, so he inserted a finger instead while his tongue went back to her clit.

Her knees spread wider as he flicked with his tongue and added a second finger to thrust several times, until they were both drenched in juices. Her throaty moans and pumping hips sped up, so he did, too. He latched his lips over her and flicked her clit as fast as he could go.

She gave several short screams as she came, clutching her breasts and pushing against his thrusting fingers. He rode the slow descent with her, keeping her warm with his mouth and hand.

She sat up enough to pull on his shoulders. "Come inside me," she breathed. "I need you to claim me before I die and go to heaven again."

"How do we do this, so I don't hurt you?" He ran his hands over her round stomach, shiny with perspiration.

She pulled a pillow from above her head and shoved it under her hips. "Try that." She smiled. "Trust me, I'll let you know if we need to do it another way."

He oozed up her, kissing her stomach and breasts as he aligned himself with her entrance. He lifted her knees, then slowly pushed into her, moaning in pleasure as her tight muscles gave just enough to fit him like a glove.

"Yes," she crooned, her eyes closed and her hips pumping. "All the way."

He pushed until he couldn't go any further, then backed out a little and thrust again. He watched her anxiously, even though it was killing him not to fully slide in and out of her wetness.

She opened her eyes and smiled. "That, only a lot harder and faster."

He thrust in and out of her like a piston, picking up

speed. Every nerve ending in his body sparked with every stroke. He rounded his back above her, so he could stay off her stomach but capture one of her distended nipples with his mouth and work it with his tongue. Pleasure swamped the mate bond, and he lost track of which sensations were his and which were hers. Her magic caressed him, magnifying every sensation.

Tingling began at the base of his spine. He fought to hold off his impending orgasm as he licked his finger, then slid his hand between them to find her clit. He slid back and forth across it, reaching through the mate bond to help her find another release. Her magic flared, her core spasmed around him as she screamed, and he was gone.

He thrust hard into her and held himself there as his orgasm blew apart any semblance of thought. The bond solidified and grabbed hold of his soul. His bear rose to the surface to finish the claiming, creating a new, shared scent for both of them. Now everyone would know he belonged to her, and she to him.

After long moments, she reached up with a shaky hand to caress his face. "That was amazing. I love you."

He slid his arms under her, then, still inside her, rolled them both so she was half on top of him. "I love you." He nuzzled her neck and savored her new scent that combined her, him, and his bear.

"I can feel the bond now. It's like a glow in my head and heart." She rolled onto her back, parting them, leaving a trail of moisture. "I think we're going to need some extra pillows. This one's wet."

He laughed and climbed over her—with a side trip for a long kiss—to the side of the bed next to the bedside table. "I'll call for some."

"May as well ask for some extra bath towels, too." She

sat up and slid to the edge of the bed. "Not to be indelicate or anything, but we both need showers." She wiped a sheen of sweat off her chest. "And I didn't eat dinner, so those damn banana Moon pies are callin' to me."

"Why don't you take a shower while I call the front desk and make some sandwiches?" He waved toward the big cooler and the bags crowded on the dresser. "Turkey? Roast beef? Ham? I didn't know what you like, so I bought one of everything. Chocolate milk, too."

"Surprise me. I like anything." She chuckled. "Well, almost anything. Our kid better be damn grateful I'm drinking milk for her." She disappeared into the bathroom.

Trevor laughed, delighted by her humor, and the fact she'd said, "our kid." He really had hit the jackpot.

After deliveries, showers, and consuming of meals and Moon pies, they made love again, more leisurely this time. He loved her confident, practical approach to pleasure, both getting and giving.

Sated, he sprawled on the big bed. The bedside clock said it was nearly midnight. She turned out the last light and crawled across the mattress toward him. The moonlight through the curtains gave him plenty of light to see by.

She rested her head on his shoulder. "Can I ask you a question?"

"Anything."

"Would you be willing to change me into a bear, after I give birth?"

He almost bolted upright in surprise. A flurry of conflicting emotions ran through him. His bear woke up and chuffed its displeasure at whatever had threatened his human half.

She sat up to look at him. Magic flared, and the bedside lamp snapped on. "Talk to me, darlin'."

He stalled for time. "Why do you want to be changed?"

"As a human, I can't protect my daughter, or even help her understand and control her dual nature. Your job takes you away a lot, so I want to be the second-biggest bear in her life." She sighed and put her hand on his chest. "Shifters live a lot longer than humans. Did you know that Shiloh's mate, Matteo, was mated once before? His human mate refused the change and died, and Matteo mourned for centuries. I don't want that for you."

Trevor shuddered at the thought of losing her. "You could become something besides my type of bear."

"Why would I want to? I love your wooly bear."

"No one else does, except my aunt. My bear isn't normal." He took her hand in his. "I'm bigger than any bear I've ever seen, and I'm the uber-alpha. No ordinary shifter can beat me in a dominance fight."

"Those all sound like pluses to me." A puzzled look settled on her face.

He caressed her hand with his thumb. "In the human world, you know how some folks are always noticing anyone with brown skin, like we might jump them or steal the silver? Double that for what most shifters, especially alphas, will think of you. All you want is to do your job, or have a cup of coffee, but they act like it's a challenge. Some of them want you out of their territory, and some, like Roehm, would want you dead." He blew out a heavy breath. "Multiply that times ten for what other bear clans will think of you. My mother and my aunt are brown bears, and my dad is a black bear. I'm a throwback of some sort. When I was fourteen, my parents sent me off to live with my aunt because I was ruining their chances for moving up in the ranks."

She tilted her head. "I haven't noticed anyone in Kotoyeesinay giving you the hairy eyeball."

"Give it time." He shook his head. "I haven't been here that long."

"To quote the really sexy man I'm madly in love with, 'Bullshit.'"

He frowned at her.

"I bet most shifters, even alphas, don't care that you're different. Especially here in Kotoyeesinay. They'd care if you caused trouble, or wanted their clan, but you don't like fighting, and you don't want to take over anything." She brushed his jaw with her fingers. "I feel your longing to be part of something. You already are. You're my mate, and the heart-father of our princess. We're a family." Through their mate bond, she sent him an image of two huge bears and a leopard cub together, surrounded by love. "That's how I see us."

Her love flooded his heart and washed away the last lonely part of him that had been expecting another rejection. He pulled her back into his arms, her thigh draped across his, her head on his chest. "Yes. To that. To everything."

She kissed his chest. "I love you."

"Want to get married tomorrow?"

She sat up again, consternation on her face. "Tomorrow, as in *tomorrow* tomorrow?"

He chuckled. "Yes, Sunday. When I asked Shiloh about a good place for a wedding, he said the heart of the glade was already booked for our commitment ceremony at four in the afternoon. He said an oracle works in the scheduling office."

He felt a hint of sadness from her. "We can wait. Oracles aren't always right."

"No, I want to, it's just that..." She slid a hand across her stomach. "My old life is gone forever, and I'm looking forward to a new life with you, but I'd always hoped my mother would be at my wedding."

"Where there's a will, there's a way, in this town." He sat up.

"I don't know." She blew out a noisy breath. "I don't want her to die of a heart attack because she thought I was dead. I think I should just call her with the news."

He knew he shouldn't ask, but he had to. "Afraid of what she'll think of me?"

"No, she'll love you, and especially the bear side of you." She looked away, then back. "I'm afraid of what she'll think of me. Pregnant. Thief. Nearly a murderer." Her hand fluttered. "She's a healing witch. She raised me to be better than that."

"If she loves you as much as you love her, she'll understand." And if she didn't, he'd be happy to personally tell her a few home truths.

Her eyes welled with tears and she smiled. "The mate bond... I heard that. It's been so long since I've had someone to stand up for me."

He knew the feeling well. He gathered her in his arms and rocked her gently.

She sniffled. "I swear I'm not usually a watering pot. Stupid hormones."

"It's okay." He kissed her forehead. "At least I'll know what to expect if we ever have another kid."

She groaned. "Let's get me through this pregnancy first." She sagged against him. Through the mate bond, he felt the wave of exhaustion that caused it.

He leaned her back onto the fresh pillows and pulled the sheet over her to block any drafts.

"So, back to my original question. Wanna get hitched tomorrow?"

"Yes," she said sleepily, patting his arm. "I hit pay sand with you. Gotta register my claim."

He chuckled. He'd never been compared to a drillable oil field before. "Yes, ma'am."

Jackie woke deliciously relaxed, for the first morning in what seemed like forever. She didn't even care that it was well past nine. Trevor had nudged her awake sometime earlier to tell her he was going out to run errands and bring back more food. She snorted with amusement as she walked by the multiple bags of food on the dresser on the way to the bathroom. Bears must like full larders.

In the shower, she started planning her day. Eat, pounce on her new mate, buy a dress, get married, invite her mate to pounce on her, and go to sleep in his arms. A far cry from her former, very structured corporate life, even though she'd been satisfied with it at the time. Funny how kidnapping, pregnancy, escaping, and falling in love could change a woman's priorities.

She felt her new mate bond energize. Trevor was close by. In case he brought company as well as food, she pulled on her sleep T-shirt, then went back to contemplating what to do with her hair. It hadn't been trimmed in months, but was still too short to pull back into anything elegant. She fluffed it to encourage it to dry, and figured she'd worry about it later.

Trevor walked in carrying a stack of containers that smelled of bacon and pastry, and a huge suitcase.

She kissed him as she took the containers from him. "Hello kisses are never going to get old."

She set the food on the chair, since they had no more table space. He put the suitcase on the bed and opened it, then stood back, watching her, with an anticipatory look on his face.

She crossed to the suitcase, which was filled with clothes. Her clothes, from her apartment in Houston. She raised an eyebrow at him. "I see that smug look on your face, cowboy. Start talkin'."

He grinned. "While you were meeting with Brooker yesterday, I asked Matteo to check your legal status in Texas. Seems your shit-for-brains ex was ducking some loan collectors and has been staying in your place, since you'd paid your lease a year in advance. He told your boss you'd had a death in the family, and that you needed more time to take care of things." He pointed toward the suitcase. "Matteo sent someone to stuff this suitcase and had it ported to Kotoyeesinay. His wedding present to you."

She laughed. "What a lovely gift." She pulled out a ruffled, cream-colored silk blouse to hold over her torso. "Most of this should even fit, if not the way it used to. I lost about twenty pounds when I was cleaning for the pride and eating frozen dinners, then gained most of it back in the last month as Princess started really growing."

She opened the closet to hang up the blouse.

"After we eat, we have a schedule for the day." He pulled a folded piece of paper out of the chest pocket of his T-shirt and handed it to her.

She opened it and puzzled over his abbreviations. "Okay, I get the wedding at four, but what are these others?"

He pointed. "The eleven-thirty is a fitting at Fairy Fineries, so I'll have something to get married in besides jeans, boots, and a shirt with snaps. They want to make a dress for you because you charmed their scissors to always stay visible in their workroom."

"But they already... oh, never mind." She'd have to work out how to do something else nice for them later.

"The one-o'clock is a trip to the real estate office, so we can choose a lot to build on. I already gave them a deposit." He rocked back on his heels and dropped his eyes. "While I was on the road, I bought plans and materials for a two-bedroom cabin. They're in my trailer." He tilted his head toward the motel's parking lot. "I wanted you and Princess to have a place to live, even if it wasn't going to be with me."

Jackie rubbed his biceps, determined not to cry. "It was always going to be with you, cowboy. You're my rock."

He smiled. "I'm glad. The three-thirty is at the town hall, for the license. We'll walk to the glade from there. They tell me there's a shortcut."

She pulled the pen out of his pocket to add a two-o'clock item to his schedule, then handed both back to him.

"What does 'N & N' stand for?"

She gave him a smart-ass smile. "Nap and nookie, of course."

The glade reminded Jackie of a botanic garden, with mossy, floral scents in the air and winding paths to show off each shrub and tree. Her frothy, fluttery red-and-pink beaded dress was right out of an epic fantasy, but her low-heeled ruby slippers were thankfully practical enough to keep her from falling on her ass.

Trevor wore an embellished deep red vest, a cream-colored tunic, and tight black pants and high, cuffed boots. He'd asked for swashbuckling, and Fairy Frocks delivered.

She squeezed Trevor's hand and pulsed her profound happiness through their mate bond, which was growing stronger with each hour. He smiled as he lifted their joined hands and kissed the back of her hand.

The path let them out into an open meadow that shimmered with sunlight and magic. Wooden plank tables mixed with white plastic deck chairs clustered toward one end. Everyone she'd met in town during the week sat or stood, chatting with many more she'd never met.

Jackie drew Trevor's attention to two women striding toward them. Trevor beamed and crossed to them quickly.

"Aunt Straya!" He kissed the beautiful black woman on her cheek. Her fitted dress had African design elements and showed her figure to advantage. He nodded to the other, much paler woman in gray whose resemblance to human was only superficial. "I'm glad you both could make it." He stepped back to put his arm around Jackie. "This is my mate and wife, Jacqueline Breton."

"Please, call me Jackie." She smiled. Any woman who could convince a teenage bear to dig her garden and chase away the critters was someone worth getting shifter parenting advice from.

"Call me Straya. Congratulations on your mate bond." She turned to motion her companion closer. "This is my friend, Auris."

Auris nodded, but kept her deep black eyes focused on Jackie's baby bump. "She is impatient."

Jackie laughed. "You're telling me." She was still getting

used to perfect strangers having something to say about her pregnancy.

"Three weeks early..." Auris held up her hand and looked at it as if she'd never seen it before. Maybe she hadn't, because it was growing thinner and turning a sickly shade of yellow. Her eyes narrowed as she turned to glare suspiciously at an empty edge of the glade. She dropped her hand and headed that direction. Where she walked, the grasses swayed away from her sandaled feet.

Trevor's wary unease mirrored Jackie's own as she looked to Straya. "Is she an oracle?"

"Maybe. I don't think she's found her final form, yet." Straya glanced at Jackie's belly, where the frilly dress displayed it proudly. "Shifter babies sometimes come early."

Trevor tightened his arm around Jackie. "We'll be ready."

"You must come visit, when your daughter is old enough to travel." She leaned closer and whispered conspiratorially. "I have pictures." She waggled her eyebrows and tilted her head to indicate Trevor.

"Don't listen to her." Trevor turned Jackie away. "Come on, there's someone who wants to see you."

Jackie laughed. "Later, Straya."

He led her to the far side of the clumps of party-goers to where a woman sat by herself at a small table.

Jackie's feet faltered. "Mama?"

Her mother's face lit up as she stood and held her arms wide open. "Jacqueline!"

Jackie stumbled into her mother's arms and wrapped her arms around her. Tears flowed as she soaked in the healing magic of her mother's love. "I missed you."

"Me, too." Her mother rubbed her shoulder. "I'm sorry I believed that lying leopard when he called from Vegas to say you and he had won a jackpot cruise around the world and were leaving the next day."

The remorse in her mother's voice made Jackie pull back to look at her. "Don't blame yourself, Mama. He's a world-class liar. I don't envy anyone who marries him."

"I should have known better." Her mother pulled out two tissues from a packet and handed one to Jackie. "You'd never have left your clients in the lurch during tax season."

Jackie chuckled. "True." She sighed. "When did you get here?"

"At noon." Her mother's eyes gleamed. "My first trip through a fairy portal." She waved fingers toward patient Trevor, standing ten feet away and undoubtedly listening to every word. "Your man called me this morning and told me everything that happened." She smiled. "He's very protective of you. He was afraid I'd disapprove of what you did to survive."

Jackie shook her head. "That was me, Mama. I wanted to be the perfect daughter so Weirtree wouldn't look down on you anymore."

"Oh, baby, you could have been a saint and it wouldn't have mattered. They were set against me the day I married your handsome father." She shrugged. "I don't give a flying fuck what they think."

Trevor snorted in surprise.

Jackie laughed. "Good." Her mother's willingness to flout expectation had always been Jackie's private delight. "What do you think of Kotoyeesinay?"

Her mother smiled. "Astounding. I had no idea..." She waved a hand to encompass the glade and the variety of species in it. "There's magic in every stone and blade of grass."

"Do you like it well enough to think about moving here

instead of Houston, like we were planning?" Jackie felt tears welling again. Damn hormones. "Trevor and I are building a house. It'll take me some time to get my finances straightened out again, after being away for so long, but I've been saving money so you could go anywhere but Weirtree."

Her mother exchanged a look with Trevor, who had sidled closer to Jackie without her noticing. "It's your surprise."

Trevor grinned. "I asked Matteo to get the Williken pride to fund an irrevocable trust for Princess, for college and stuff. Matteo went above and beyond to, uhm, extract two more, one for your mother and one for you, as the injured family." From out of the wide bag hanging on his belt, he took out two folded pieces of paper and handed it to her. "Have a look."

The figure on the page took her breath away. "That's... wow." The education fund amount on the second page made her grin like a village idiot. "Princess could buy her own college."

Tears spilled down her cheeks. Trevor took the papers back from her and handed her a tissue.

"Sorry." Thank the goddess she'd decided against wearing any makeup for the day.

Her mother patted her shoulder. "It only gets worse. Wait'll delivery."

Jackie laughed. "Gee, thanks, Mama."

"Don't worry. I'll be here when the time comes. And yes, I'll think about moving here. I want to know my granddaughter." She hugged Jackie again. "I think that elven woman dressed in *Gelsemium sempervirens* wants to start."

The ceremony was short and sweet. Guivre herself, resplendent in green vines with yellow flowers, acted as celebrant. She bound their hands together with a strand of spider web. "As you have already dedicated yourselves to one another in the shifter way, all that is left for me is to wish you a long life filled with health and happiness. The strength of love is not just the grand, but the small—the tiny gestures, the quiet thoughts, the anticipation of needs. Your children will feel it and learn from you, and all the world will be the better for it."

She waved two fingers. The spider web settled into the skin of their wrists, making a complicated knotwork pattern before it vanished. Jackie felt the wave of subtle but powerful magic course through her, and she knew Trevor felt it, too. "Now you will always know where the other is, in this world or any other."

Guivre splayed her fingers, and the shaded glade lit up with thousands of pinpoint lights. "I, for one, would like some fairy sundew." She pointed to the table with a stack of full champagne glasses. "First round is on me."

The attendees laughed and cheered as Trevor drew Jackie into his arms for a passionate kiss that left her no doubt what they'd be doing as soon as possible.

Before they could step away, Guivre touched Jackie's forearm. "The glade welcomes you and accepts your pledge of defense. Talk to Iolo Maxen about honing your talent for making talismans. You're a natural, and your talent will grow with time." She touched Trevor's hand. "The glade also welcomes you and accepts your pledge of defense. It's been too long since we've had an Ice Age shifter gracing our presence. We are honored."

"A what?" asked Trevor.

"An *Arctotherium*. From what is now called South

America. Even ogres would hesitate to take on a bear of your size, with those claws." Guivre cocked her head, and subtle magic flared. "I see. Your parents were imbeciles to drive you off." She shook her head. "Regular shifters of this age instinctively fear you because you're a predator of predators. Corrupt alphas like Roehm fear you most of all, because not even magic can make you submit." Guivre smiled. "You are a gift of your moon goddess, born in mystery in times of need. Your mate will be, too, when you change her."

Trevor frowned. "Whose magic? My mother's? She says she doesn't have any, that Aunt Straya got it all."

Jackie narrowed her eyes. "Whose need?"

Guivre nodded at Jackie. "The world's. Extraordinary beings for extraordinary challenges." She smiled slightly. "Unfortunately, the unseen gods are always coy as to what those challenges are, until after the fact."

Jackie rolled her eyes. "Just like politicians."

Guivre laughed, and the glade echoed with the tiny shimmer of bells. "Yes, very like." She stepped back and waved toward the guests. "Go celebrate with your families and make new friends."

She turned and stepped daintily toward the red wyvern, who was crouching in the trees. She spoke in an unfamiliar language. The wyvern lowered his big head to the ground. There was something sad and soulful in the opalescent eyes.

Jackie slipped her hand into Trevor's and felt the mate bond spring to life. "Come on, handsome, let's do as we've been told." She moved closer and gave him a provocative smile full of sin. "After that, I'm planning on a wild ride or two on my cowboy."

He laughed as he scooped her and her amazing dress up

into his arms and kissed her, then spun her in a circle. "You're killing me here."

She laughed. "Right back at you, cowboy."

He set her back down on the ground and slipped his hand in hers.

She felt a familiar urge and sighed. "Do you suppose the glade heart has a place to pee?"

Thank you for reading *Shifter Mate Magic*, the first story in the Ice Age Shifters series. If you liked it, please post a quick review, so other readers can enjoy it, too.

There are more stories in the Ice Age Shifters series. Sign up for my newsletter at http://bit.ly/CVN-news so you won't miss finding out about tnew books.

Thanks to my brave and honest beta readers and typo hunters, my professional editor Shelley Holloway, my talented cover designer Amanda Kelsey, and my equally talented sketch artist Sam Salas.

The Ice Age Shifters series:

- *Shifter Mate Magic (Book 1)*
- *Shift of Destiny (Book 2)*
- *Heart of a Dire Wolf (Book 3)*
- *Dire Wolf Wanted (Book 4)*

FREE EXCERPT FROM SHIFT OF DESTINY (ICE AGE SHIFTERS BOOK 2)

NUNN, COLORADO ~ SUMMER ~ PRESENT DAY

MOIRA GRAHAM LOCKED the door of her old, noisy, beater of a car out of habit, not because anyone sane would steal it. She was too tired and hot to sweep out the back, where barley cake pellets had fallen. It could wait until the cooler morning hours. She wiped the sweat off her forehead, then resettled her dusty ball cap over her equally dusty hair and pushed her braid back. The heat of the almost-summer June day was finally letting up with the setting sun, but her T-shirt was still clinging to her like she'd gone swimming in it.

The walk to the cozy outbuilding she temporarily called home always seemed twice as far after a long day at work. At least she had a job, even if it meant she never had a day off. That was fair, she supposed, since the dairy cows she cleaned stalls for didn't get days off, either. She slung her backpack over one shoulder as she walked up the narrow sidewalk, past the neat, white clapboard house that fronted the street.

"Moira!"

She jumped, then turned to face the elderly, dark-haired woman coming around the corner of the house.

"You've got to stop sneaking up on me like that," Moira said loudly. Del, her landlady, refused to wear her hearing aids in public because she said they made her look old. As a consequence, conversations with her involved a lot of shouting.

Del wiped her soapy hands on the dishtowel she was carrying. "I went to the sheriff's office this afternoon. You were right about that man who interviewed Emilio and his friends for that magazine sales job. The attorney general's office said he has charges pending in about five other states. He's even stranded whole teams in strange towns with no way to get back home."

"Oh no. Those poor kids." She'd overheard the guy interviewing Emilio and two other teenagers in the town's park—who conducted evening interviews at a picnic table? —and had a hunch the man was a slimeball, because his body language hadn't matched his words or his oily smiles. In the dappled shade, he'd almost looked like he had the scales of a snake. She'd mentioned it to Del, who'd started making calls. Slimeball wasn't the half of it, apparently. She shook her head. "I'm sorry the job didn't work out."

Small towns in the northeastern plains of Colorado had very few jobs for recent high-school graduates like Del's live-in grandson. Moira had lucked into her current job because she happened to know how to catch runaway cows. The barn work was exhausting, but it paid in cash under the table, which was exactly what she needed. Neither she nor her diary farm employer wanted a paper trail. Moira paid cash to rent the tiny house, because Del didn't want a paper trail, either.

Del eyed the clear bag in Moira's hand that held a wrapped sandwich and chips. "Fast food is bad for you. Come on in. I made a big pot of chili."

Moira shook her head. "No thanks, I just need a shower and to put my feet up. I don't think I sat once all day." She didn't want to take advantage of Del's generous nature. Her landlady's only income besides social security was renting out the illegally converted shed, and she had still-unemployed Emilio to feed.

Del gave her a sly look. "You should use some of your magic and get yourself a boyfriend to give you a foot massage every night." Del knew everyone in Nunn and the surrounding farms and ranches, and had been trying to pair Moira up with anyone remotely eligible. Del had loved her husband dearly, and thought everyone should have the chance at that kind of happiness.

Moira had given up trying to tell her that any kind of relationship wasn't in the cards, and just laughed. "I keep telling you, it's not magic. I just notice things."

Del patted Moira's arm. "I understand, sweetie. It'll be our little secret."

Moira suppressed a sigh. People who wanted magic to be real never let facts get in the way of a good belief. She looked at her watch. "You're going to miss your favorite show if you stand here gabbing with me."

"You're a good girl." Del gave Moira a quick hug. "Go take your shower."

Del trundled off, leaving Moira to follow the narrow walk that led to her tiny home. At twenty-nine, Moira was too old to be called a girl, though maybe Del applied the term to anyone under fifty.

In the backyard, Moira stopped to admire Del's lovingly tended garden. It reminded her of her foster mother's garden, which had been filled with practical vegetables, but still had room for a few flowers. She missed her foster parents a great deal, but couldn't risk dragging them into the mess that was her life. All she could do was send occasional postcards and breezily tell them she was still enjoying her road trip of three years and counting. Maybe in another year, if things stayed quiet, she could finally go home again for a while.

Moira straightened her slumped shoulders, then turned and opened the screen door to the converted outbuilding.

Nothing fell.

The pink petunia petal she'd carefully placed between the door and the frame when she'd left at dawn was lying in the dirt. She picked it up and gently brushed the dust off with her thumb. The petal felt like someone had stomped on it, and incongruously smelled a bit like wet dog.

She tried the door's handle, and was relieved to find it locked as she'd left it. She let herself in with the key and pulled the door closed behind her. Sunlight streamed in from high west windows as she took in the room.

The chair at the square, battered pub table was perfectly centered under it, and the table was perfectly aligned with the strip of a kitchen. The microwave and toaster oven on the counter both squared up perfectly with the edge. The square, mosaic-mirrored vase was perfectly aligned with the edge of the low bookshelf. She'd bet her sandwich that the contents of her medicine cabinet would be too neat and that the few things hanging in the repurposed school locker that was her wardrobe were now evenly spaced.

Lawrence Witzer had not only found her, he'd been in her house and pawed through her things.

Moira allowed herself three swear words that wouldn't count toward her swear fund.

Hell. That was her life since meeting the man, turning him down, and evading him ever after. She was sorry she had ever taken that summer job three years ago as a costumed fortune teller for a Renaissance fair in southern Colorado, doing entertainment tarot readings for the visitors.

Wealthy but crazy Witzer had visited her tent once and become convinced she was a genuine psychic, not just someone with common sense and a vivid imagination, which had gotten her into trouble since childhood. She'd spun him a vague but colorful tale of business setbacks, intrigue, and ultimate victory over an enemy, because richly dressed customers like him tipped better when they were the hero of the story. She'd had no idea who he was at the time, only that he had expensive taste in jewelry and a compulsive need for order. He'd come back several more times over the run of the fair for additional readings. Then on the last day, he'd astonishingly invited her to interview for a job as a business analyst for international financial deals. He was undeterred when she admitted she only had an associate's degree in hospitality, and she'd only gotten that to please her family.

She'd been flattered by the attention and the breathtaking salary Witzer had offered, but his behavior during the meeting in Denver, in the hotel's presidential suite, was deeply weird. He obsessively straightened everything, even her sweater on the back of her chair, without seeming to be aware he was doing it. He asked her nonsensical questions about her "magical gifts," mumbled in a foreign language, and watched her like he expected her to sprout antennae or spontaneously combust. His expression made her imagine he'd soon ask to look at her ankles and teeth, like she was a prize thoroughbred he wanted to buy.

She'd told him she needed to think about it and escaped quickly, then sent him a polite email a week later declining his offer, after she'd lined up a tour guide job in Vermont because she wanted to see the fall foliage. Instead of dropping it, he'd seemed to take her refusal as a challenge, which he'd since carried to extremes. He'd overshot "eccentric" some time ago and was now well into obsessive-delusional.

Shit. She knew from experience that after Witzer, his goons with strong arms and black vans would soon be at her door. They'd come after dark this time, because they'd learned from their encounter last year that she could scream really loud, a skill she'd developed when she'd played a banshee in a haunted house. Something told her that if she didn't leave in the next thirty minutes, she could kiss her freedom goodbye. She was certain that Witzer, based on his unflagging pursuit of her, had no intention of letting her get away again.

She put her backpack on her chair and pulled out the battered rolling suitcase from the locker wardrobe. She put her toiletries in a plastic bag in the bottom, so her clothes wouldn't be ruined by leaks. Her worn athletic shoes went next, followed by her hanging clothes, then her spare pair of jeans and T-shirts, then her underwear, bras, and socks for easy access. She'd have to carry her winter coat and snow boots. She'd learned to keep her computer and cash with her at all times, so they were already in her backpack, along with her cellphone charger, hoodie, tools, first-aid kit, hair brush and small mirror, and the few important papers she had. She shoved her sandwich and chips into the top of the backpack.

In the kitchen, she pulled the can opener out of the drawer, along with one set of eating utensils and the plug-in immersion heater, and stuffed them in her backpack's front pocket. She put her only can of stew in the backpack's side pocket. She pulled the comforter off her futon and zipped it up to make it a sleeping bag again, stuffed it with her thrift-store sheets and pillow, then rolled it up. That was her entire life packed in fifteen minutes. She looked around for anything she couldn't live without.

Fuckity fuck, fuck, fuck. Same word, so it was still exempt from the swear fund. She really liked the quaint little town of Nunn and its residents who admired her for staying off the grid, even though they thought it was by choice rather than necessity. The dairy farm owed her a week's pay that she'd never see, and Del would be hurt that Moira didn't say goodbye. She was heartily sick of the life of a tumbleweed, blown by the wind and Witzer's demented desire to harness her supposed gifts for his benefit.

Speaking of the wind, she needed a direction. She pulled the well-worn US roadmap out of her backpack and spread it out on the narrow futon. She placed the bruised flower petal on her palm and blew it gently toward the map. It almost seemed to sparkle in the streaming late-afternoon sun, then landed. The petal's tip pointed to a mountain town on the southern Wyoming border called Kotoyeesinay. It was as good a choice as any, though the route to get there from Nunn looked convoluted. Perhaps it would slow down Witzer's hunters, trying to guess where she'd gone. If she was lucky, she could be there in a day.

Continue the adventure in SHIFT OF DESTINY